Alfred Walls

**The oldest drama in the world, the book of Job : arranged in
dramatic form with elucidations**

Alfred Walls

The oldest drama in the world, the book of Job : arranged in dramatic form with elucidations

ISBN/EAN: 9783337306144

Printed in Europe, USA, Canada, Australia, Japan

Cover: Foto ©Andreas Hilbeck / pixelio.de

More available books at **www.hansebooks.com**

THE OLDEST DRAMA
IN THE WORLD

THE BOOK OF JOB

ARRANGED IN DRAMATIC FORM WITH ELUCIDATIONS

By REV. ALFRED WALLS

WITH A PREFATORY NOTE

BY HENRY A. BUTTZ, D.D., LL.D.

President of Drew Theological Seminary

———— · · ◆ · · ————

NEW YORK: HUNT & EATON
CINCINNATI: CRANSTON & STOWE
1891

PREFATORY NOTE.

IT affords me pleasure to commend to the reader the valuable work of Rev. Alfred Walls on the Book of Job.

The Book of Job is worthy of reading with deepest interest in any form as a part of the sacred Scriptures, but Mr. Walls has given to the whole narrative a vividness which adds greatly to the interest of the reader. While many may take exception to the dramatic form in which it has been cast by the editor, all will agree that the mode of presentation is unique and worthy of careful attention. Some will read this work for the peculiarity of its setting; all should read it for the interest and instruction it affords.

HENRY A. BUTTZ.

CONTENTS.

THE OLDEST DRAMA IN THE WORLD.

THE Book of Job is a literary treasure-house! Where can its magnificent soliloquies, its prayers, and its varied descriptions be equaled? The soliloquies are the finest in literature; the descriptions are unique; the prayers are from the breaking heart.

There is enough in this drama to fire the enthusiasm of genius. It is the very thesaurus of elocutionists. There are parts which, rendered with impassioned voice and action, thrill us from head to foot. The Booths, Garrick, Kemble, and Irving never found richer material. Here can be seen and heard the absorbed expression of soliloquy, the stir of refutation, the voice and attitudes of petition when it has become desperation.

Imagery revels upon its chaste pages, and pictorial ideas are strewn freely before the reader. Nature and thought, space and stars are laid under tribute by the actors. •Objects far and near move in panoramic gloom or splendor; birds build their nests or soar heavenward; lions spring upon their prey; "Aha!" snorts the war-horse at the voice of the trumpet; leviathan trails behind him his shining wake; clouds drop their rain or are turned here and there at the behest of God; the pillars of heaven tremble; the foundation of the earth is laid, and the line is stretched upon it; rains descend, floods destroy, lightnings flash, and thunders roar; seas cover the trembling dead, and constellations are led forth. What can equal the grandeur of the bursting storm in Act IV, of Job's stoicism there, and Elihu's terrified expressions? Especially in the last act God speaks from above the scenes with incomparable sublimity.

If we judge the Book of Job by a purely literary standard, two of the *dramatis personæ* are, indeed, daring creations—these are God and Satan.

JOB.

The book has but one great human character; it bears his name. Compare Job with a Hamlet, a Richard the Third, or a Lear; he is more sharply defined than any. Job is a masterpiece. He bears the theme of the book in himself. There is not a moment, from the beginning to the end of the drama, from the first words of the prologue to the last words of the epilogue, that he does not engage our sympathy and command our thought. The three friends and Elihu are expedients to keep our interest upon the hero of the solitary struggle—a struggle in which he is beset by his disease, by his memory of better days, by the loss of property and children, by his conviction that God has been unjust to him and has deserted him, by his isolation from all friends who understand him, by the horror every innocent man must feel of going down to death with a pure character and an outcast's name.

THE THREE FRIENDS.

Why do Job's friends importune him so often and so persistently? Because they are not common friends. Seven days and seven nights they watch his silent grief, and with wonderful etiquette do not speak to him. Afterward, in seven scenes, they implore him to repent of the sins which their theology forces them to believe he has committed. Amid all their confusion and their irritability they cannot let him suffer on so long as they believe they can persuade him to repent and thus behold his restoration to health and prosperity. Job having done no evil can repent of none. O rare but misguided friends! They pursue him not that they may hurt, but that they may save him.

ELIHU.

Elihu steps forward as a mediator, but he retires apparently unsuccessful.

OBJECTION.

The mistaken objection that the Book of Job is not a drama may arise from the fact that in other dramas the conversational part allotted to each actor is much briefer than the long speeches of Job and his friends. A man crushed by tremendous losses and sorrow and physical torment, whose very bones were burning with heat and racked with pain, would scarcely speak with conversational brevity; on the contrary, after seven days and seven nights of speechless grief, his agonized utterance would burst forth in a flood; should a friend then unjustly accuse him, he would rouse himself to prolonged and plaintive remonstrance, mingled with entreaty, accusations, warnings, argument, and personal defense.

The speeches of Job's friends are natural, though they are highly wrought. Expostulation with an alert and healthy offender might be less lengthy, but discourse is longer with the helpless who are supposed to be culpably unfortunate. It is noticeable that the utterances of the three friends, and of Elihu, are not argument only, or views merely; they criminate, they suggest, they entreat, they warn, they betray personal irritability.

This composition is more than a colloquy or a philo-
sophical expression of views, for Job and his friends are
represented as actually suffering, as censuring a person
present. Job suffers before their eyes. Their speech is
often aimed directly at him. He answers from *the midst
of his woes.* Job differs, intrinsically, from all other
dramas, because no other exhibits such scenes.

The author ranks above Shakespeare, Racine, Molière,
or Goethe; and he probably wrote before the Greek
founders of tragedy and comedy were born. Shakespeare
is the loftiest of our modern dramatic peaks, but beyond
him, and remote, with massive top bathed in the morning
light of antiquity and inspiration, stands a loftier summit.
It is probable nature never will upheave another such em-
inence. Well, then,

Who Wrote the Drama?

Strange to say, no one knows. Some critics suppose
that it is one of the works of that Solomon the king
whose proverbs were three thousand, and whose songs
were a thousand and five. Other scholars say that it is
one of the works of the same Moses who wrote the Penta-
teuch ; that he wrote it during his forty years of shepherd
life, to which he fled with a trained mind and a love for
letters. Others hold that Job himself or one of the
prophets wrote it. We are unaware, consequently,

When it was Written.

The drama is historical, doubtless founded upon the
sufferings of a real Job in the land of Uz. Unquestion-
ably written between the time of Moses and one thousand
years later, yet in that millennium it is impossible to fix any
century to which it belongs. No historical fact is more
assured than that the book existed at least five hundred

years before Mary, in the stable at Bethlehem, looked upon the face of her immortal Son.

WHERE WAS IT WRITTEN?

This also has not been determined with certainty, but as it was written in the Hebrew language, and found among the Hebrew Scriptures, and quoted by Hebrew writers, we may conjecture fairly it was written in, or not far from, Palestine. As "the language approximates more closely to Arabic than that of any other Hebrew work, and is replete with Chaldaisms," Arabia or Chaldea may have been the home of the author who wrote it. But the book is with us, and not a jot the worse for its unknown authorship, for its unknown birthplace, and for its unknown date.

THE THEME IS DIVINE PROVIDENCE.

It is the only book in the Bible so entirely devoted to the subject of divine providence; and as the subject is the profoundest of subjects, the drama is the profoundest of dramas.

The author was doubtless prompted to write the drama against the prevailing error in even the trained minds of his time, which was probably long after Job's day. The representatives of the false doctrine are Job's three friends.

The arguments of Eliphaz, Bildad, and Zophar are summed up in this: Affliction is sent only upon the wicked. These friends believe Job to have been wicked secretly. Elihu presents a broader view—that God sometimes afflicts men for their good (yet Elihu, too, unfortunately, believes Job to be guilty). Job refutes the superficial error of the three, but will not, or cannot, answer the more advanced argument of Elihu.

God speaks in the last act, but he does not explain his

providence.   Yet Act V, Scenes I, II, is *more* than sarcasm
and a declaration of power.   These are declarations concerning his creation—another form of the same lesson
which Christ gave in his Sermon on the Mount: If God
so clothe the *grass* and the *lily* and feed the *birds*, he will
care for human creatures who serve him.

God leaves many questions unanswered, and neither
does he in this drama, nor does Christ in his Sermon on
the Mount, reveal their answer.

The writer is zealous to show us that the ills inflicted
upon Job were of Satan.   The Lord neither robbed him
of his property, nor killed his children, nor smote his
body.   God's part in this drama is beneficent.   He de-
stroys nothing.   He gave Job twice as much as he had
lost.

Job's deliverance is signal and beautiful.

God did not abandon Job; he only permitted him to be
severely tried—the drama is not a heartless tragedy.

JOB'S TRIAL.

Perhaps, with one exception, no such trial has ever been
recorded.

The woes of Job are dreadful to contemplate.

Poor lone Job!   He descends the steps of hope, flight
after flight.   He feels himself descending.   Faith shines
by instants only.   It is life and death, up and down, rays
and gloom, then total blackness.   He struggles hard, then
gives up; struggles again, and loses heart.   He entreats
his friends for sympathy, then drives them away.   He is
a bird without a song, a world without a sun!

Job's struggle was upward.   His physical condition had
much to do with his irritable temper.   He took no wicked
pleasure in accusing God.   When despair flung him to the

earth his longing heart ever clamored after the Being to whom he had often sacrificed; he still loved the favor of God, and his averted face filled his soul with death. Satan and misguided good men could not destroy his love for integrity, or by accusation cause him to confess fellowship with guilt. Job was an imprisoned bird, whose wings were weak not because they were unused; they were unfeathered and sore from ceaseless beatings against the wires which kept them from flying up toward God.

Over-zealous good men did what Satan had not done without them; they augmented his affliction and his despair, and with good intentions turned the scale. Rebellious words against God do not come forth until he is seated with the three friends before him, and is tested by the slow fires of their suspicion.

Job, when he was in trouble, did not foresee the last scene or read the epilogue of this drama. He did not hear fourteen thousand sheep bleating in his vast folds; nor see six thousand she-asses bearing his burdens, and filling his dairies, or grazing in his meadows; nor one thousand oxen plowing his fields, or treading out his enormous harvests; nor six thousand camels swinging rapidly across the deserts, re-exalting his influence and re-extending his traffic to many lands; nor dream of the joyous shouts of his multitudes of shepherds and herdmen and drivers and tillers of his soil; nor see in his house the richly clad servants who were to await, in silence, his lordly commands. He did not see the graceful forms of Jemimah, Keziah, and Keren-happuch moving about his parlors, and the pillars of his temple-home, his seven stalwart and godly sons. His wife and servants were yet driven away by his loathsomeness. He was in the bottom of a pit never penetrated by starlight! Only at times his vista held a bright vision. Job was yet a wail—a sob!

The crisis turns favorably while Job prays for his friends. From that moment he begins to emerge from his desolation. He leaves the ash-heap, the potsherd, and the sackcloth forever. He walks into his life again with one hundred and forty happy years before him.

It is interesting to notice that God did not tell Job he would grant him prosperity; from the drama also it is impossible to think that Job was ever told of the interviews with that malignant being who primarily caused all his sorrows.

There is an Arabian legend which says that Job suffered seven years.

The rulers of heaven and hell watched him in his misery.

THE SCENES.

Bible scholars have long agreed that the controversies, prayer, and soliloquies in Acts III and IV could not have occurred at one sitting. I have taken the liberty to arrange them as they are found in the several scenes of this book. In fixing nearly all the scenes plausibility has been almost my only determinative. However, I think it is certain that Scene I, Act I, and Scene I, Act II, are not in heaven, but on the earth. The expression "sons of God" refers to good men, and not to angels or to heavenly councillors. (See also Gen. vi, 4.) It is improbable that Satan, or any evil being, could so wantonly invade heaven on any evil errand. So far as I know the arrangement in dramatic form which follows is the first since the drama was written upon the scroll of its unknown author.

TEXTUAL CHANGES.

The changes made in the text are not mine, but are those suggested by the American Old Testament Revisers.

The changes are printed separately in this book, and may be examined by all—the new version in hand.

THE BIBLIOGRAPHY

has been expressly prepared for " The Oldest Drama in the World " by the Rev. S. G. Ayres, Assistant Librarian of Drew Theological Seminary. It is given in an appendix.

ALFRED WALLS.

Drew Theological Seminary, Madison, N. J.

ANALYSIS.

THE Book of Job is about as long as Shakespeare's "Hamlet." Like that drama it has five acts, which are arranged in twenty-one scenes :

PROLOGUE: JOB. (Chapter i, 1–5.)

ACT I. (Chapter i, 6–22.)

Scene I. Interview between God and Satan concerning Job.

Scene II. Result of interview—Job's loss of property and children announced by four messengers.

Scene III. Result of announcement—Job worships.

ACT II. (Chapter ii, 1–10.)

Scene I. Second interview between God and Satan concerning Job.

Scene II. Result of second interview—Job appears, smitten with boils—Job's wife speaks.

ACT III. (Chapter ii, 11–xxxii, 1.)

PROLOGUE: ELIPHAZ, BILDAD, AND ZOPHAR.

Scenes I.—X. The appearance of the three friends. They sit with him upon the ground seven days and seven nights. After Job has spoken, Eliphaz begins the controversy. The friends appear in nine of the ten scenes of this act, in seven of which they are, for a short time, in controversy with Job. They believe he must have sinned or such evil could not have come upon him.

2

They urge him to repent that he may be restored to prosperity. He stoutly disclaims any offense against God.

This act also exhibits a frightful struggle of the *soul* against despair.

Act IV.   (Chapter xxxii, 2–xxxvii, 24.)

Prologue: Elihu.

Scene I.   Elihu appears; rebukes the three and Job—He urges Job to repent, and endeavors to overthrow some statements Job has made in Act III.

Scene II.   Elihu alone remains with Job during a terrible storm, still urging him to repent.

Act V.   (Chapter xxxviii–xlii, 11.)

Scenes I and II.   God speaks, and humbles Job by the declaration of his wisdom and power.

Scene III.   God rebukes Eliphaz.

Postlogue.

Scene IV.   Job in prosperity, surrounded by his friends.

Epilogue.   (Chapter xlii, 12–17.)

The opening Prologue and the Epilogue are, of course, extremes, the latter representing Job twice as prosperous as before his affliction. The Epilogue is a blast of trumpets.

DRAMATIS PERSONÆ.

THE LORD.

SATAN.

JOB, a wealthy Sheik.

JOB's WIFE.

ELIPHAZ, prince and scholar of Teman, ⎫
BILDAD, prince and scholar of Shuah, ⎬ Three friends of Job.
ZOPHAR, prince and scholar of Naamah, ⎭

ELIHU, a young prince and scholar of Buz.

Field-hand, ⎫
Shepherd, ⎬ Four messengers.
Drover, ⎪
Household Servant, ⎭

Sons of God (human worshipers), Job's brethren, sisters, and acquaintance.

PROLOGUE.

THERE was a man in the land of Uz, whose name was Job; and that man was perfect and upright, and one that feared God, and turned away from evil.

And there were born unto him seven sons and three daughters.

His substance also was seven thousand sheep, and three thousand camels, and five hundred yoke of oxen, and five hundred she-asses, and a very great household; so that this man was the greatest of all the children of the East.

And his sons went and held a feast in the house of each one upon his day; and they sent and called for their three sisters to eat and to drink with them.

And it was so, when the days of their feasting were gone about, that Job sent and sanctified them, and rose up early in the morning, and offered burnt-offerings according to the number of them all: for Job said, "It may be that my sons have sinned, and renounced God in their hearts." Thus did Job continually.

ACT I.

Scene I.   *A Place of Worship: Worshipers Assembled.*[1]

Enter Satan.[2]

The Lord.[3] Whence comest thou?

Satan.[4] From going to and fro in the earth,
And from walking up and down in it.

The Lord.[3] Hast thou considered my servant Job?
For there is none like him in the earth,
A perfect and an upright man,
One that feareth God and turneth away
From evil.

Satan.[4] Doth Job fear God for nought?
Hast thou not made an hedge about him,
And about his house,
And about all that he hath, on every side?
Thou hast blessed the work of his hands, and
His substance is increased in the land.
But put forth thine hand now,
And touch all that he hath, and
He will renounce thee to thy face.

The Lord.[3] Behold, all that he hath
Is in thy power; only upon himself
Put not forth thine hand.

[*Exit Satan,*[5] *the worshipers still unconscious of his visit.*]

---

[1] " Now it came to pass on the day, when the sons of God came to present themselves before the Lord,"

[2] " That Satan came also among them."

[3] " And the Lord said unto Satan," etc.

[4] " Then Satan answered the Lord, and said," etc.

[5] " So Satan went forth from the presence of the Lord."

SCENE II.   *Probably in Job's House.*

JOB *sitting quietly in magnificence.   A storm passing away.*[1]

Enter First Messenger.[2]

First Messenger. The oxen were plowing,
And the asses feeding beside them : and
The Sabeans fell upon them,
And took them away;
Yea, they have slain the servants with the edge of the
    sword ;   [*Enter Second Messenger.*[3]
And I only am escaped alone to tell thee.

Second Messenger. The fire of God is fallen from heaven,
And hath burned up the sheep, and
The servants, and consumed them ;

                              [*Enter Third Messenger.*[3]
And I only am escaped alone to tell thee.

Third Messenger. The Chaldeans made three bands, and
Fell upon the camels,
And have taken them away,
Yea, and slain the servants with the edge of the sword ;

                              [*Enter Fourth Messenger.*[3]
And I only am escaped alone to tell thee.

---

[1] The messengers in this scene enter in great excitement and drenched with rain by the storm through which they came. The fire from heaven, which consumed the sheep, and the wind from the wilderness, which smote the four corners of the house, were perhaps the lightning and the cyclone of one storm.—*A. W.*

[2] " And it fell on a day when his sons and his daughters were eating and drinking wine in their eldest brother's house, that there came a messenger unto Job, and said," etc.

[3] " While he was yet speaking, there came also another, and said," etc.

Fourth Messenger. Thy sons and thy daughters
Were eating and drinking wine
In their eldest brother's house :
And, behold, there came a great wind
From the wilderness,
And smote the four corners of the house,
And it fell upon the young men, and they are dead ;
And I only am escaped alone to tell thee.   [*Exeunt.*

SCENE III.   *On Job's Grounds.*

Enter JOB, *having rent his mantle and shaved his head.
He prostrates himself in deep dejection.*[1]

Job. Naked came I out of my mother's womb,
And naked shall I return thither :

[*Then, trustfully.*

The Lord gave, and the Lord hath taken away ;
Blessed be the name of the Lord.

[*End of Act I.*

IN ALL THIS JOB SINNED NOT :
NOR CHARGED GOD FOOLISHLY.

---

[1] "Then Job arose, and rent his mantle, and shaved his head, and fell down
upon the ground, and worshiped ; and he said," etc.

ACT II.

SCENE I. *A Place of Worship: Worshipers*[1] *Assembled.*

Enter[2] SATAN.

The Lord.[3] Whence comest thou?
Satan.[4] From going to and fro in the earth,
And from walking up and down in it.
The Lord.[3] Hast thou considered my servant Job?
For there is none like him in the earth,
A perfect and an upright man,
One that feareth God, and
Turneth away from evil: and he
Still holdeth fast his integrity,

---

[1] "Again it came to pass on the day when the sons of God came to present themselves before the Lord,

[2] "That Satan came also among them to present himself before the Lord.

[3] "And the Lord said unto Satan," etc.

[4] "And Satan answered the Lord, and said," etc.

Although thou movedst me against him,
To destroy him without cause.

   Satan.[1] Skin for skin, yea, all that a man hath
Will he give for his life.
But put forth thine hand now, and touch
His bone and his flesh,
And he will renounce thee to thy face.

   The Lord.[2] Behold he is in thine hand; only spare his
      life.

[*Exit Satan,*[3] *worshipers unconscious of his visit, as before.*

SCENE II.   *Near Job's House.*

JOB *sitting in ashes and scraping himself with a potsherd.*[4]
JOB'S WIFE *appears.*

Job's wife.[5] Dost thou still retain thine integrity?
Renounce God, and die.

   Job.[6] Thou speakest as one of the foolish
Women speaketh.
What? shall we receive good
At the hand of God, and shall we not receive evil?

                [*Exeunt.*

IN ALL THIS DID NOT JOB SIN WITH HIS LIPS.

---

[1] " And Satan answered the Lord, and said," etc.
[2] " And the Lord said unto Satan," etc.
[3] "So Satan went forth from the presence of the Lord,
    And smote Job with sore boils from the sole of his foot unto his crown."
[4] " And he took a potsherd to scrape himself withal;
    And he sat among the ashes."
[5] " Then said his wife unto him," etc.
[6] " But he said unto her," etc.

PROLOGUE TO ACT III.

NOW when Job's three friends heard of all this evil
    That was come upon him,
They came every one from his own place;
Eliphaz the Temanite, Bildad the Shuhite, and
Zophar the Naamathite:
And they made an appointment together
To come to bemoan him and to comfort him.

ACT III.

SCENE I. *Open Country. Highway Stretching into the Distance.*

Enter JOB, *carrying his potsherd; himself the incarnation of woe.* The Three Friends *appear on the highway.*
(And when they lifted up their eyes afar off,
And knew him not,
They lifted up their voice, and wept;
And they rent every one his mantle,
And sprinkled dust upon their heads toward heaven.)

                                [*Exit Job, followed by the Three.*

SCENE II. *A More Secluded Spot.*

JOB *sitting in ashes:* the Friends *seated at some distance.*[1]
Day and night come and go seven[2] *times during this melancholy scene. Then the afflicted speaks.*[3]

  Job. Let the day perish wherein I was born,
And the night which said,
"There is a man child conceived."
  Let that day be darkness;
  Let not God from above seek for it,
  Neither let the light shine upon it.

---

[1] "So they sat down with him upon the ground"
[2] "Seven days and seven nights,
    And none spake a word unto him:
    For they saw that his grief was very great."
[3] "After this Job opened his mouth
    And cursed his day.
    And Job answered and said," etc.

Let darkness and the shadow of death claim it for their
    own;
Let a cloud dwell upon it;
Let all that maketh black the day terrify it.
As for that night, let thick darkness seize upon it:
Let it not rejoice among the days of the year;
Let it not come into the number of the months.
Lo, let that night be barren;
Let no joyful voice come therein.
Let them curse it that curse the day,
Who are ready to rouse up leviathan.
Let the stars of the twilight thereof be dark:
Let it look for light, and find none;
Neither let it behold the eyelids of the morning:
Because it shut not up the door of my mother's womb,
Nor hid trouble from mine eyes.

              [*Turns in agony to his friends.*

Why died I not from the womb?
Why did I not give up the ghost when my mother bare me?
Why did the knees receive me?
Or why the breasts, that I should suck?
For now should I have lien down and been quiet;
I should have slept; then had I been at rest:
With kings and counselors of the earth,
Which built up waste places for themselves;
Or with princes that had gold,
Who filled their houses with silver:
    Or as a hidden untimely birth
I had not been;
As infants which never saw light.
There the wicked cease from troubling;
And the weary be at rest.
There the prisoners are at ease together;

They hear not the voice of the task-master.
The small and the great are there;
And the servant is free from his master.

                       [*The friends do not answer.*

Wherefore is light given to him that is in misery,
And life unto the bitter in soul;
Which long for death, but it cometh not;
And dig for it more than for hid treasures;
Which rejoice exceedingly,
And are glad, when they can find the grave?
    Why is light given to a man whose way is hid,
And whom God hath hedged in?
For my sighing cometh before I eat,
And my groanings are poured out like water.
For the thing which I feared cometh upon me,
And that which I am afraid of cometh unto me.
I am not at ease, neither am I quiet, neither have I rest;
But trouble cometh.   [*Exeunt.*

SCENE III.   *On Job's Grounds.*

JOB *alone.*

Enter ELIPHAZ, BILDAD, *and* ZOPHAR.   *Prolonged silence.*

  Eliphaz [*to Job*].[1] If one assay to commune with thee,
    wilt thou be grieved?
But who can withhold himself from speaking?

Behold, thou hast instructed many,
And thou hast strengthened the weak hands.
Thy words have upholden him that was falling,
And thou hast made firm the feeble knees.

---

[1] "Then answered Eliphaz the Temanite, and said," etc.

But now it is come unto thee, and thou faintest ;
It toucheth thee, and thou art troubled.
Is thy fear of God thy confidence,
And the integrity of thy ways thy hope ?   . [*No answer.*

Remember, I pray thee, who ever perished, being innocent ?
Or where were the upright cut off ?   [*Still no answer.*

According as I have seen, they that plow iniquity,
And sow trouble, reap the same.
By the breath of God they perish,
And by the blast of his anger are they consumed.
The roaring of the lion, [1] and the voice of the fierce lion,
And the teeth of the young lions, are broken.
The old lion perisheth for lack of prey,
And the whelps of the lioness are scattered abroad.

[*Eliphaz, attributing to pride Job's restlessness over this
    insinuated accusation, changes his tactics and en-
    deavors to humble him.*

Now a thing was secretly brought to me,
And mine ear received a whisper thereof.
In thoughts from the visions of the night,
When deep sleep falleth on men,
Fear came upon me, and trembling,
Which made all my bones to shake.
Then a spirit passed before my face ;
The hair of my flesh stood up.
It stood still, but I could not discern the appearance thereof ;
A form was before mine eyes :
There was silence, and I heard a voice, saying,
                              [*Quotes the Apparition.*

---

[1] The lion is here taken as a type of *evil-doers.*

" Shall mortal man be more just than God?
Shall a man be more pure than his Maker?
Behold, he putteth no trust in his servants;
And his angels he chargeth with folly:
How much more them that dwell in houses of clay,
Whose foundation is in the dust,
Which are crushed before the moth!"

> [*Eliphaz confirms the speech of the Apparition.*

Betwixt morning and evening they are destroyed:
They perish forever without any regarding it.
Is not their tent-cord plucked up within them?
They die, and that without wisdom.

Call now; is there any [1] that will answer thee?
And to which of the holy ones wilt thou turn?

For vexation killeth the foolish man,
And jealousy slayeth the silly one.
I have seen the foolish taking root:
But suddenly I cursed his habitation.
His children are far from safety,
And they [2] are crushed in the gate,
Neither is there any to deliver them.
Whose harvest the hungry eateth up,
And taketh it even out of the thorns,
And the snare gapeth for their substance.
For affliction cometh not forth of the dust,
Neither doth trouble spring out of the ground;
But man is born into trouble,
As the sparks fly upward.   [*More kindly.*

---

[1] That is, any except God.
[2] Eliphaz thus cruelly reminds Job of his children.

But as for me, I would seek unto God,
And unto God would I commit my cause:
Which doeth great things and unsearchable;
Marvelous things without number:
Who giveth rain upon the earth,
And sendeth waters upon the fields:
So that he setteth up on high those that be low;
And those which mourn are exalted to safety.
He frustrateth the devices of the crafty,
So that their hands cannot perform their enterprise.
He taketh the wise in their own craftiness:
And the counsel of the froward is carried headlong.
They meet with darkness in the daytime,
And grope at noonday as in the night.
But he saveth from the sword of their mouth,
Even the needy from the hand of the mighty.
So the poor hath hope,
And iniquity stoppeth her mouth. [*With greater sympathy.*

Behold, happy is the man whom God correcteth:
Therefore [*to Job*] despise not thou the chastening of the
    Almighty.
For he maketh sore, and bindeth up;
He woundeth, and his hands make whole.
He shall deliver thee in six troubles;
Yea, in seven there shall no evil touch thee.
In famine he shall redeem thee from death;
And in war from the power of the sword.
Thou shalt be hid from the scourge of the tongue;
Neither shalt thou be afraid of destruction when it cometh.
At destruction and dearth thou shalt laugh;
Neither shalt thou be afraid of the beasts of the earth.
For thou shalt be in league with the stones of the field;

And the beasts of the field shall be at peace with thee.
And thou shalt know that thy tent is in peace ;
And thou shalt visit thy fold, and shalt miss nothing.
Thou shalt know also that thy seed shall be great,
And thine offspring as the grass of the earth.
Thou shalt come to thy grave in a full age,
Like a shock of corn cometh in in its season.
Lo this, we have searched it, so it is ;
Hear it, and know thou it for thy good.

   Job.[1] O that my vexation were but weighed,
And all my calamity laid in the balances !
For now it would be heavier than the sand of the seas :
Therefore [*addressing his friends*] have my words been
     rash.
For the arrows of the Almighty are within me,
The poison whereof my spirit drinketh up :
The terrors of God do set themselves in array against me.
Doth the wild ass bray when he hath grass ?
Or loweth the ox over his fodder ?
       [*Proceeds to notice what Eliphaz has said.*
Can that which hath no savor be eaten without salt ?
Or is there any taste in the white of an egg ?
My soul refuseth to touch *them;* [*The sayings of Eliphaz*
They are loathsome meat to me.
       [*Job is here diverted by his despair.*
O that I might have my request ;
And that God would grant *me* the thing that I long for !
Even that it would please God to crush me ;
That he would let loose his hand and cut me off !
And be it still my consolation ;
Yea, let me exult in pain that spareth not :

[1] "Then Job answered and said," etc.

3

That I have not [*as they suppose*] denied the words of the
    Holy One.   [*Pauses, defiant.*

What is my strength, that I should wait?
And what is mine end,[1] that I should be patient?
Is my strength the strength of stones?
Or is my flesh of brass?
Is it not that I have no help in me,
And that wisdom is driven quite from me?
                        [*Rebukes Eliphaz.*

To him that is ready to faint kindness should be showed
    from his friend;
Even to him that forsaketh the fear of the Almighty.
            [*Job's mind returns to his own brethren.*

My brethren have dealt deceitfully as a brook,
As the channel of brooks that pass away;
Which are black by reason of the ice,
And wherein the snow hideth itself:
What time they wax warm, they vanish:
When it is hot, they are consumed out of their place.
The caravans that travel by the way of them turn aside;
They[2] go up into the waste, and perish.
The caravans[3] of Tema looked,[4]
The companies of Sheba waited for them.
They were ashamed because they had hoped;
They came thither, and were confounded.
                    [*Job turns upon the Three.*

For now ye are nothing;
Ye see a terror, and are afraid.

---

[1] He evidently did not expect to recover, therefore why do anything?
[2] The caravans.
[3] Doubtless referring to real incidents well known to the friends.
[4] For such streams.

Did I say,
Give unto me; or,
Offer a present for me of your substance; or,
Deliver me from the adversary's hand; or,
Redeem me from the hand of the oppressors?
> [*They cannot say that he had asked these things.*

Teach me, and I will hold my peace:
And cause me to understand wherein I have erred.

[*Embarrassment among the friends. As they cannot tell
him wherein, he goes on with scathing sarcasm.*

How forcible are words of uprightness!
But your reproof, what doth it reprove?
Do ye think to reprove words?
Seeing that the speeches of one that is desperate are as wind.
Yea [*with withering contempt*], ye would cast lots upon
the fatherless,
And make merchandise of your friend.
Now therefore be pleased to look upon me;
For surely I shall not lie to your face.   [*Drives them off*.
Return, I pray you, let there be no injustice;
Yea, return again; my cause is righteous.
Is there injustice on my tongue?
Cannot my taste discern mischievous things?
> [*Exeunt Eliphaz, Bildad, Zophar.*

> [*Job, left alone, falls into a soliloquy.*

Is there not a warfare to man upon earth?
And are not his days like the days of an hireling?
As a servant that earnestly desireth the shadow,
And as an hireling that looketh for his wages:
So am I made to possess months of vanity,
And wearisome nights are appointed to me.
When I lie down, I say,

"When shall I arise and the night be gone?"
And I am full of tossings to and fro unto the dawning of
     the day.
My flesh is clothed with worms and clods of dust;
My skin closeth up and breaketh out afresh.
My days are swifter than a weaver's shuttle,
And are spent without hope.

                                                      [*Prays.*

O remember that my life is a breath:
Mine eye shall no more see good.
The eye of him that seeth me shall behold me no more:
Thine eyes shall be upon me, but I shall not be.
As the cloud is consumed and vanisheth away,
So he that goeth down to Sheol[1] shall come up no more.
He shall return no more to his house,
Neither shall his place know him any more.

     Therefore I will not refrain my mouth;
I will speak in the anguish of my spirit;
I will complain in the bitterness of my soul.
Am I a sea, or a sea-monster,   [*Complains.*
That thou settest a watch[2] over me?
When I say,
"My bed shall comfort me,
My couch shall ease my complaint;"
Then thou scarest me with dreams,
And terrifiest me through visions:
So that my soul chooseth strangling,
And death rather than these my bones.

     I loathe my life; I would not live alway:
Let me alone; for my days are vanity.
What is man, that thou shouldest magnify him,

---

[1] The grave.
[2] Eliphaz, Bildad, and Zophar.

And that thou shouldest set thy mind upon him,
And that thou shouldest visit him every morning,
And try him every moment?
How long wilt thou not look away from me,
Nor let me alone till I swallow down my spittle?
If I have sinned, what do I unto thee, O thou watcher of
    men?
Why hast thou set me as a mark for thee,
So that I am a burden to myself?
And why dost thou not pardon my transgression, and take
    away mine iniquity?   *[In profound despair.*
For now shall I lie down in the dust;
And thou shalt seek me diligently, but I shall not be.
                                      [Exit.

SCENE IV.   *On Job's Grounds.*

JOB *alone.*

Enter BILDAD, ELIPHAZ, *and* ZOPHAR.

Bildad.[1] How long wilt thou speak these things?
And how long shall the words of thy mouth be like a
    mighty wind?
Doth God pervert judgment?
Or doth the Almighty pervert justice?
  If thy children have sinned against him,
And he have delivered them into the hand of their trans-
    gression.

If thou wouldest seek diligently unto God,
And make thy supplication[2] unto the Almighty;

---

[1] "Then answered Bildad the Shuhite, and said," etc.
[2] Bildad evidently does not know that Job has prayed. See Act III, Scene III.

If thou wert pure and upright;
Surely now he would awake for thee,
And make the habitation of thy righteousness prosperous.
And though thy beginning was small,
Yet thy latter end should greatly increase.
　　For inquire, I pray thee, of the Former Age,
And apply thyself to that which their fathers have searched
　　　out :
(For we are but of yesterday, and know nothing,
Because our days upon earth are a shadow :)
Shall not they teach thee, and tell thee,
And utter words out of their heart ?

Can the rush grow without mire ?
Can the flag grow without water ?
While it is yet in its greenness, and not cut down,
It withereth before any other herb.
So are the paths of all that forget God ;
And the hope of the godless man shall perish :
Whose confidence shall break in sunder,
And whose trust is a spider's web.
He shall lean upon his house, but it shall not stand :
He shall hold fast thereby, but it shall not endure.
He is green before the sun,
And his shoots go forth over his garden.
His roots are wrapped about the stone-heap,
He beholdeth the place of stones.
　　If he be destroyed from his place,
Then it shall deny him, saying,
" I have not seen thee."
　　　　　　　　　　　　　　　[*With sarcasm.*

Behold, this is the joy of his way,
And out of the earth shall others spring.

[Speaks more kindly.

Behold, God will not cast away a perfect man,
Neither will he uphold the evil-doers.
He will yet fill thy mouth with laughter,
And thy lips with shouting.
They that hate thee shall be clothed with shame;
And the tent of the wicked shall be no more.

    Job.[1] Of a truth I know that it is so:
But how can a man be just with God?
If he be pleased to contend with him,
He cannot answer him one of a thousand.

    He is wise in heart, and mighty in strength:
Who hath hardened himself against him, and prospered?

    Which removeth the mountains, and they know it not,
When he overturneth them in his anger.

    Which shaketh the earth out of her place,
And the pillars thereof tremble.

    Which commandeth the sun, and it riseth not;
And sealeth up the stars.

    Which alone stretcheth out the heavens,
And treadeth upon the waves of the sea.

    Which maketh the Bear, Orion, and the Pleiades,
And the chambers of the south.

    Which doeth great things past finding out;
Yea, marvelous things without number.

    Lo, he goeth by me, and I see him not:
He passeth on also, but I perceive him not.

    Behold, he seizeth the prey, who can hinder him?
Who will say unto him,
" What doest thou?"

[Rebelliously.

God will not withdraw his anger;

---

[1] "Then Job answered and said," etc.

The helpers of Rahab do stoop under him.
How much less shall I answer him,
And choose out my words to reason with him?
Whom, though I were righteous, yet would I not answer;
I would make supplication to mine adversary.

      [Yet Job instantly changes, and accuses God.

If I had called, and he had answered me;
Yet would I not believe that he hearkened unto my voice.
For he breaketh me with a tempest,
And multiplieth my wounds without cause.
He will not suffer me to take my breath,
But filleth me with bitterness.

If we speak of strength, lo, he is mighty!
And if of judgment:
"Who," saith he, "will summon me?"   [me:
Though I be righteous, mine own mouth shall condemn
Though I be perfect, it shall prove me perverse.

      [Then, in desperation at this thought.

I am perfect; I regard not myself;
I despise my life.
It is all one; therefore I say,
   He destroyeth the perfect and the wicked.
   If the scourge slay suddenly,
   He will mock at the trial of the innocent.
   The earth is given into the hand of the wicked:
   He covereth the faces of the judges thereof;
If it be not he, who then is it?   *[Awkward pause.*

                       [Exeunt the Three.

                          [Job prays.

Now my days are swifter than a post:
They flee away, they see no good.

They are passed away as the swift ships:
As the eagle that swoopeth on the prey.
 If I say, I will forget my complaint,
I will put off my sad countenance, and be of good cheer,
[Then] I am afraid of all my sorrows,
I know that thou wilt not hold me innocent.
I shall be condemned;
Why then do I labor in vain?
If I wash myself with snow water,
And make my hands never so clean;
Yet thou wilt plunge me in the ditch,
And mine own clothes shall abhor me.

[Job soliloquizes.

For he is not a man, as I am, that I should answer
    him,
That we should come together in judgment.
There is no daysman betwixt us,
That might lay his hand upon us both.
Let him take his rod away from me,
And let not his terror make me afraid:
Then would I speak, and not fear him;
For I am not so in myself.
My soul is weary of my life;
I will give free course to my complaint;
I will speak in the bitterness of my soul.
I will say unto God:

[Prays.

Do not condemn me!
Show me wherefore thou contendest with me.
Is it good unto thee that thou shouldest oppress,
That thou shouldest despise the work of thine hands,
And shine upon the counsel of the wicked?
 Hast thou eyes of flesh,

Or seest thou as a man seeth?
Are thy days as the days of man,
Or thy years as man's days,
That thou inquirest after mine iniquity,
And searchest after my sin,
Although thou knowest that I am not wicked;
And there is none that can deliver out of thine hand?

Thine hands have framed me and fashioned me
Together round about; yet thou dost destroy me.
Remember, I beseech thee, that thou hast fashioned me as
    clay;
And wilt thou bring me into dust again?
Hast thou not poured me out as milk,
And curdled me like cheese?
Thou hast clothed me with skin and flesh,
And knit me together with bones and sinews.
Thou hast granted me life and favor,
And thy visitation hath preserved my spirit.

Yet these things thou didst hide in thine heart;
I know that this is with thee:
    If I sin, then thou markest me,
And thou wilt not acquit me from mine iniquity.
    If I be wicked, woe unto me;
And if I be righteous, yet shall I not lift up my head ·
Being filled with ignominy
And looking upon mine affliction.
And if my head exalt itself, thou huntest me as a lion:
And again thou showest thyself marvelous unto me.
Thou renewest thy witnesses against me,
And increaseth thine indignation upon me;
    Changes and warfare are with me.

Wherefore then hast thou brought me forth out of the
     womb?
I had given up the ghost, and no eye had seen me.
I should have been as though I had not been;
I should have been carried from the womb to the grave.
Are not my days few? cease then,
And let me alone, that I may take comfort a little,
Before I go whence I shall not return,
Even to the land of darkness and of the shadow of death;
The land dark as midnight;
The land of the shadow of death, without any order,
And where the light is as midnight.   *[Exit.*

Scene V. *On Job's Grounds.*

Job *alone.*

Enter Zophar, Bildad, Eliphaz, *and* Elihu.

Zophar.[1] Shall not the multitude of words be answered?
And should a man full of talk be justified?
Should thy boastings make men hold their peace?
And when thou mockest, shall no man make thee ashamed?

For thou sayest:
" My doctrine is pure,
And I am clean in thine eyes."

But O that God would speak,
And open his lips against thee;
And that he would show thee the secrets of wisdom,
For he is manifold in understanding!

Know therefore that God exacteth of thee less than thine
iniquity deserveth.

Canst thou by searching find out God?
Canst thou find out the Almighty unto perfection?
It is high as heaven; what canst thou do?
Deeper than Sheol; what canst thou know?
The measure thereof is longer than the earth,
And broader than the sea.
If he pass through, and shut up,
And call unto judgment, then who can hinder him?
For he knoweth vain men:

---

[1] " Then answered Zophar the Naamathite, and said," etc.

He seeth iniquity also, even though he consider it not.
  But vain man is void of understanding,
  Yea, man is born as a wild ass's colt.

If thou set thine heart aright,
And stretch out thine hands toward him;
If iniquity be in thine hand, put it far away,
And let not unrighteousness dwell in thy tents;
Surely then shalt thou lift up thy face without spot;
Yea, thou shalt be steadfast, and shalt not fear:
For thou shalt forget thy misery;
Thou shalt remember it as waters that are passed away:
And thy life shall be clearer than the noonday;
Though there be darkness, it shall be as the morning.
And thou shalt be secure, because there is hope;
Yea, thou shalt search about thee, and shalt take thy rest
        in safety.
Also thou shalt lie down, and none shalt make thee afraid;
Yea, many shall make suit unto thee.

But the eyes of the wicked shall fail,
And they shall have no way to flee,
And their hope shall be the giving up of the ghost.

  Job.[1] No doubt but ye are the people,
        And wisdom shall die with you.
But I have understanding as well as you;
I am not inferior to you:
Yea, who knoweth not such things as these?

                          [*On the one hand.*
  I am as one that is a laughing-stock to his neighbor.

---

[1] " Then Job answered and said," etc.

I who called upon God, and he answered :
The just and the perfect man is a laughing-stock.

   (In[1] the thought of him that is at ease there is contempt
      for misfortune ;
   It is ready for them whose foot slippeth.)

                         [*On the other hand.*

The tents of robbers prosper,
And they that provoke God are secure ;
Into whose hand God bringeth abundantly.

                        [*Turns to Zophar.*

But ask now the beasts, and they shall teach thee ;
And the fowls of the air, and they shall tell thee :
Or speak to the earth, and it shall teach thee ;
And the fishes of the sea shall declare unto thee.

   Who knoweth not in all these, [*Alluding to his afflictions.*
That the hand of the Lord hath wrought this ?
In whose hand is the soul of every living thing,
And the breath of all mankind.

                [*With sarcasm Job continues.*

Doth not the ear try words,
Even as the palate tasteth its meat ?
With aged men is wisdom,
And in length of days is understanding.
With him is wisdom and might ;
He hath counsel and understanding.
   Behold, he breaketh down, and it cannot be built again :
   He shutteth up a man, and there can be no opening.
   Behold, he withholdeth the waters, and they dry up ;
   Again, he sendeth them out, and they overturn the earth.

---

[1] Something in the friends' manner doubtless calls him to say warningly the words in parentheses.

With him is strength and wisdom ;
The deceived and the deceiver are his.
> [*Showing God's use of his power and wisdom.*

He leadeth counselors away spoiled,
And judges maketh he fools.

He looseth the bond of kings,
And bindeth their loins with a girdle.

He leadeth priests away spoiled,
And overthroweth the mighty.

He removeth the speech of the trusty,
And taketh away the understanding of the elders.

He poureth contempt upon princes,
And looseth the belt of the strong.

He discovereth deep things out of darkness,
And bringeth out to light the shadow of death.

He increaseth the nations, and he destroyeth them :
He enlargeth the nations, and he leadeth them captive.

He taketh away understanding from the chiefs of the
people of the earth,
And causeth them to wander in a wilderness where there
is no way.

They grope in the dark—without light !—
And he maketh them to stagger like a drunken man.
> [*Further discussion useless.*

Lo, mine eye hath seen all this,
Mine ear hath heard and understood it.
What ye know, the same do I know also :
I am not inferior to you.

Surely I would speak to the Almighty,
And I desire to reason with God.
But ye are forgers of lies,

[Scornfully.

Ye are physicians of no value.
O that ye would altogether hold your peace,
And it should be your wisdom!

Hear now my reasoning,
And hearken to the pleadings of my lips.
   Will ye speak unrighteously for God,
And talk deceitfully for him?
Will ye show partiality to him?
Will ye contend for God?
Is it good that he should search you out?
Or as one deceiveth a man, will ye deceive him?
He will surely reprove you,
If ye show partiality.
Shall not his majesty make you afraid,
And his dread fall upon you?   *[Silence.*

Your memorable sayings are proverbs of ashes,
Your defenses are defenses of clay.   *[Contemptuously.*
Hold your peace, let me alone, that I may speak,
And let come on me what will.   *[Defiantly.*
Wherefore should I take my flesh in my teeth,
And put my life in mine hand?   *[Despairs.*
Behold he will slay me; I have no hope!
Nevertheless I will maintain my ways before him.
This also shall be my salvation,   *[When He shall come.*
That a godless man shall not come before him!
   [Job emphatically and formally asserts his innocence.
Hear diligently my speech,
And let my declaration be in your ears:
   Behold now I have ordered my cause;

I know that I am righteous.
Who is he that will contend with me?
[*Seeing that nothing can be done with Job at this interview,*
[*Exeunt the Three.*[1]

For now shall I hold my peace and give up the ghost.

Only do not two things unto me.   [*Prays.*
Then will I not hide myself from thy face:
   Withdraw thine hand far from me;
And let not thy terror make me afraid.
Then call thou, and I will answer;
Or let me speak, and answer thou me.
   How many are mine iniquities and sins?
Make me to know my transgression and my sin.
   Wherefore hidest thou thy face,
And holdest me for thine enemy?

Wilt thou harass a driven leaf?
And wilt thou pursue the dry stubble?
For thou writest bitter things against me,
And makest me to inherit the iniquities of my youth:
Thou puttest my feet also in the stocks, and markest all my
     paths;
Thou settest a bound to the soles of my feet:
Though I am like a rotten thing that consumeth,
Like a garment that is moth-eaten.

   Man that is born of woman
Is of few days, and full of trouble.
He cometh forth like a flower, and is cut down:
He fleeth also as a shadow, and continueth not.

---

[1] Elihu remains. See chap. xiii, 27; xxxiii, 8-11.

4

And dost thou open thine eyes upon such an one,
And bringest me into judgment with thee?
Who can bring a clean thing out of an unclean? not one.
Seeing his days are determined, the number of his months
      is with thee,
And thou hast appointed his bounds that he cannot pass;
Look away from him, that he may rest,
Till he shall accomplish, as an hireling, his day.
For there is hope of a tree, if it be cut down, that it will
      sprout again,
And that the tender branch thereof will not cease.
Though the root thereof wax old in the earth,
And the stock thereof die in the ground;
Yet through the scent of water it will bud,
And put forth boughs like a plant.
But man dieth, and is laid low:
Yea, man giveth up the ghost, and where is he?
As the waters fail from the sea,
And the river wasteth and drieth up;
So man lieth down and riseth not:
Till the heavens be no more, they shall not awake,
Nor be roused out of their sleep.
O that thou wouldest hide me in Sheol,
That thou wouldest keep me secret, until thy wrath be
      past,
That thou wouldest appoint me a set time, and remember
      me!
[*As he prays does Job for a moment doubt even his im-
      mortality?*
   If a man die, shall he live again?
All the days of my warfare would I wait,
Till my release should come.
Thou shouldest call, and I would answer thee:

Thou wouldest have a desire to the work of thine hands.
But now thou numberest my steps :   [*Dejectedly.*
Dost thou not watch over my sin ?
My transgression is sealed up in a bag,
And thou fastenest up mine iniquity.

And surely the mountain falling cometh to nought,
And the rock is removed out of its place ;
The waters wear the stones ;
The overflowings thereof wash away the dust of the earth :
So thou destroyest the hope of man.
Thou prevailest forever against him, and he passeth ;
Thou changest his countenance, and sendest him away.
His sons come to honor, and he knoweth it not ;
And they are brought low, but he perceiveth it not of
        them.

But his flesh upon him hath pain,
And his soul within him mourneth !   [*Exit Job.*

Scene VI. *On Job's Grounds.*

Job *alone.*

Enter Eliphaz, Bildad, *and* Zophar.

Eliphaz.[1] [*To Job.*] Should a wise man make answer
    with vain knowledge,
And fill his belly with the east wind?
Should he reason with unprofitable talk,
Or with speeches wherewith he can do no good?

---

[1] "Then answered Eliphaz the Temanite, and said," etc.

Yea, thou doest away with fear,
And restrainest devotion[1] before God.
For thine iniquity teacheth thy mouth,
And thou choosest the tongue of the crafty.
Thine own mouth condemneth thee, and not I;
Yea, thine own lips testify against thee.

Art thou the first man that was born?
Or wast thou brought forth before the hills?
Hast thou heard the secret counsel of God?
And dost thou limit wisdom to thyself?
What knowest thou, that we know not?
What understoodest thou, which is not in us?
With us are both the gray-headed and the very aged men,
Much elder than thy father.
Are the consolations of God too small for thee.
Even the word that is gentle toward thee?

    [Job betrays anger and Eliphaz rebukes him.
Why doth thine heart carry thee away?
And why do thine eyes flash?
That thou turnest thy spirit against God,
And lettest such words go out of thy mouth.

     [Eliphaz speaks contemptuously.
What is man, that he should be clean?
And he which is born of a woman, that he should be
  righteous?
Behold, he putteth no trust in his holy ones;
Yea, the heavens are not clean in his sight.
How much less one that is abominable and corrupt,
A man that drinketh iniquity like water!

---

[1] Eliphaz does not know that Job has already prayed. Act III, Scenes III,
IV, V.

I will show thee, hear thou me;
And that which I have seen I will declare:
(Which wise men have told
From their fathers, and have not hid it;
Unto whom alone the land was given,
And no stranger passed among them:)
   The wicked man travaileth with pain all his days,
Even the number of years that are laid up for the op-
     pressor.
A sound of terrors is in his ears;
In prosperity the spoiler shall come upon him:
He believeth not that he shall return out of darkness,
And he is waited for of the sword.
He wandereth abroad for bread, saying,
" Where is it?"
He knoweth that the day of darkness is ready at his
     hand:
Distress and anguish make him afraid;
They prevail against him, as a king ready to the battle:
Because he stretched out his hand against God,
And behaveth himself proudly against the Almighty;
He runneth upon him with a stiff neck,
With the thick bosses of his bucklers:
Because he hath covered his face with his fatness,
And gathered fat upon his loins;
And he hath dwelt in desolate cities,
In houses which no man inhabited,
Which were ready to become heaps.
He shall not be rich, neither shall his substance continue,
Neither shall their possessions be extended on the earth.
He shall not depart out of darkness;
The flame shall dry up his branches;
And by the breath of his mouth shall he go away.

Let him not trust in vanity, deceiving himself :
For vanity shall be his recompense.
It shall be accomplished before his time,
And his branch shall not be green.
He shall shake off his unripe grape as the vine,
And shall cast off his flower as the olive.
For the company of the godless shall be barren,
And fire shall consume the tents of bribery.
They conceive mischief, and bring forth iniquity,
And their belly prepareth deceit.

Job.[1] I have heard many such things :
Miserable comforters are ye all.
Shall vain words have an end ?
[*To Eliphaz.*] Or what provoketh thee that thou an-
     swerest ?
I also could speak as ye do ;
If your soul were in my soul's stead,
I could join words together against you,
And shake mine head at you.
But I would strengthen you with my mouth,
And the solace of my lips should assuage your grief.
                      [*Exeunt the Three.*
[*Job rises, and, pacing to and fro, soliloquizes petulantly.*
Though I speak, my grief is not assuaged :
And though I forbear, what am I eased ?
But now he hath made me weary !
[*Addresses God.*] Thou hast made desolate all my company.
And thou hast laid fast hold on me, which is a witness
     against me :
And my leanness riseth up against me, it testifieth to my
     face.

----

[1] " Then Job answered and said," etc.

> *[Resumes his soliloquy.*

He [God] hath torn me in his wrath, and persecuted me ;
He hath gnashed upon me with his teeth :
Mine adversary sharpeneth his eyes upon me.

> *[Thinks resentfully of his friends just gone.*

They have gaped upon me with their mouth ;
They have smitten me upon the cheek reproachfully ;
They gather themselves together against me.

> *[Thinks God has abandoned him.*

God delivereth me to the ungodly,
And casteth me into the hands of the wicked.
I was at ease, and he brake me asunder !
Yea, he hath taken me by the neck, and dashed me to pieces !
He hath also set me up for his mark.
His archers compass me round about,
He cleaveth my reins asunder, and doth not spare ;
He poureth out my gall upon the ground.
He breaketh me with breach upon breach ;
He runneth upon me like a giant.

> *[Thinks he suffers undeservedly and in spite of praying.*

I have sewed sackcloth upon my skin,
And laid my horn[1] in the dust.
My face is foul with weeping,
And on my eyelids is the shadow of death ;
Although there is no violence in mine hands,
And my prayer is pure.
O earth, cover not thou my blood,
And let my cry have no resting-place !

Even now, behold, my witness is in heaven,
And he that voucheth for me is on high. *[Weeps bitterly.*

---

[1] Horn, an emblem of power and honor; a change from dignity to disgrace is here contrasted.

My friends scorn me :
But mine eye poureth out tears unto God ;
That he would maintain the right of a man with God,
And of a son of man with his neighbor!
For when a few years are come, [at longest,]
I shall go the way whence I shall not return.
My spirit is consumed, my days are extinct,
The grave is ready for me.
Surely there are mockers[1] with me,
And mine eye dwelleth upon their provocation.[2]   [*Prays.*

Give now a pledge, be surety for me with thyself ;
Who is there that will strike hands with me ?
For thou hast hid their heart from understanding :
Therefore[3] shalt thou not exalt them.
He that denounceth his friends for a prey,
Even the eyes of his children shall fail.
                         [*Resumes his soliloquy.*
But he hath made me also a byword of the people ;
And they spit in my face!
                    [*Thinks of his physical condition.[4]*
Mine eye also is dim by reason of sorrow,
And all my members are as a shadow.
    Upright men shall be astonied at this,
And the innocent shall stir up himself against the godless.

---

[1] Referring to his friends Eliphaz, Bildad, and Zophar.

[2] That is, " I can see very well how they would provoke me ! "

[3] Job's prayer drifts into condemnation of his three friends.

[4] Delitzsch says ; " The description of this [Job's] disease calls to mind Deut. xxviii, 35 with 27, and is, according to the symptoms mentioned . . . in the book, *elephantiasis* (so called because the limbs become jointless lumps like elephant's legs). . . . The disease begins with the rising of tubercular boils, and at length resembles a cancer spreading itself over the whole body, by which the body is so affected that some of the limbs fall completely away. Scraping with a potsherd will not only relieve the intolerable itching of the skin, but also remove the matter."

                              [Pauses and reflects.

Yet shall the righteous hold on his way,

And he that hath clean hands shall wax stronger and stronger.

        [Sees the Three at a distance, and calls sarcastically.

But return ye—all of you—and come now!

And I shall not find a wise man among you!

                [Resumes his soliloquy dejectedly.

    My days are past, my purposes are broken off,

Even the thoughts of my heart.

They change the night into day:

The light, say they, is near unto the darkness.

    If I look for Sheol as mine house;

If I have spread my couch in the darkness;

If I have said to corruption,

" Thou art my father;"

To the worm,

" Thou art my mother, and my sister;"

Where then is my hope?   *[Despairs.*

And as for my hope, who [else] shall see it?

It shall go down to the bars of Sheol,

When once there is rest for me in the dust.   *[Exit.*

SCENE VII. *Near Job's House.*[1]

JOB *alone.*

Enter BILDAD, ZOPHAR, *and* ELIPHAZ; BILDAD *remonstrating with the Two.*

Bildad.[2] How long will ye lay snares for words?
[*To Job.*] Consider, and afterward we will speak.

                           [*A long pause.*

Wherefore are we accounted as beasts,
And are become unclean in your sight?
Thou that tearest thyself in thine anger,
Shall the earth be forsaken for thee?
Or shall the rock be removed out of its place?

                          [*Resumes the argument.*

Yea, the light of the wicked shall be put out,
And the spark of his fire shall not shine.
The light shall be dark in his tent,
And his lamp above him shall be put out.
The steps of his strength shall be straitened,
And his own counsel shall cast him down.
For he is cast into a net by his own feet,
And he walketh upon the toils.
A gin shall take him by the heel,
And a snare shall lay hold on him.
A noose is hid for him in the ground.
And a trap for him in the way.
   Terrors shall make him afraid on every side,
And shall chase him at his heels.
His strength shall be hunger bitten,
And calamity shall be ready at his side.

---

[1] See xviii, 21 ; xix, 15, 16.
[2] "Then answered Bildad the Shuhite, and said," etc.

The members of his body shall be devoured,
Yea, the first-born of death shall devour his members.
He shall be rooted out of his tent wherein he trusteth;
And he shall be brought to the king of terrors.

There shall dwell in his tent that which is none of his:
Brimstone shall be scattered upon his habitation.
His roots shall be dried up beneath,
And above shall his branch be cut off.

His remembrance shall perish from the earth,
And he shall have no name in the street.
He shall be driven from light into darkness,
And chased out of the world.

He shall have neither son nor son's son among his people,
Nor any remaining where he sojourned.
They that come after shall be astonied at his day,
As they that went before were affrighted.
Surely such are the dwellings of the unrighteous,
And this is the place of him that knoweth not God.

Job.[1] How long will ye vex my soul,
And break me in pieces with words?
These ten times have ye reproached me:
Ye are not ashamed that ye deal hardly with me.
And be it indeed that I have erred,
Mine error remaineth with myself.

          [Blames God for all his trouble.

If indeed ye will magnify yourselves against me,
And plead against me my reproach:
Know now that God hath subverted me in my cause,
And hath compassed me with his net.

          [Pathetically continues to accuse God.

Behold, I cry out of wrong, but I am not heard:

---

[1] "Then Job answered and said," etc.

I cry for help, but there is no judgment.
He hath fenced up my way that I cannot pass,
And hath set darkness in my paths.
He hath stripped me of my glory,
And taken the crown from my head.
He hath broken me down on every side, and I am gone:
And mine hope hath he plucked up like a tree.
He hath also kindled his wrath against me,
And he counteth me unto him as one of his adversaries.
His troops come on together, and cast up their way
    against me,
And encamp round about my tent.

    [*Kinsfolk, friends, and servants have abandoned him.*
He hath put my brethren far from me,
And mine acquaintance are wholly estranged from me.
My kinsfolk have failed,
And my familiar friends have forgotten me.
  They that dwell in mine house, and my maids, count
    me for a stranger:
I am an alien in their sight.
I call unto my servant, and he giveth me no answer,
Though I entreat him with my mouth.
  My breath is strange to my wife,
And my supplication to the children of mine own mother.
Even young children despise me;
If I arise, they speak against me.
All my inward friends abhor me:
And they whom I loved are turned against me.
  My bone cleaveth to my skin and to my flesh,
And I am escaped with the skin of my teeth.
                  [*Cries out for sympathy.*
Have pity upon me, have pity upon me, O ye my
    friends;

For the hand of God hath touched me.
Why do ye persecute me as God,
And are not satisfied with my flesh?

> [*Then rises to the heights of hope.*

O that my words were now written!
O that they were inscribed in a book!
That with an iron pen and lead
They were graven in the rock forever!
But as for me, I know that my redeemer liveth,
And at last he shall stand up upon the earth:
And after my skin, even this body is destroyed,
Then without my flesh shall I see God:
Whom I, even I, shall see on my side,
And mine eyes shall behold, and not as a stranger.

> [*Sudden terrible anguish, and this awful cry.*

My reins are consumed within me!

> [*When he has recovered his breath, enraged he turns upon his friends.*

If ye say, "How we will persecute him!"
And that the root of the matter is found in me;
Be ye afraid of the sword:
For wrath bringeth the punishments of the sword,
That *ye* may know there is a judgment.

Zophar.[1] Therefore do my thoughts give answer to
me,
Even by reason of my haste that is in me.
I have heard the reproof which putteth me to shame,
And the spirit of my understanding answereth me.

> [*Takes up the controversy.*

Knowest thou not this of old time,

---

[1] "Then answered Zophar the Naamathite, and said," etc.

Since man was placed upon earth,
That the triumphing of the wicked is short,
And the joy of the godless but for a moment?
    Though his excellency mount up to the heavens,
And his head reach unto the clouds;
Yet he shall perish forever like his own dung:
They which have seen him shall say, "Where is he?"
He shall fly away as a dream, and shall not be found:
Yea, he shall be chased away as a vision of the night.
The eye which saw him shall see him no more;
Neither shall his place any more behold him.
His children shall seek the favor of the poor,
And his hands shall give back his wealth.
His bones are full of his youth,
But it shall lie down with him in the dust.
    Though wickedness be sweet in his mouth,
Though he hide it under his tongue;
Though he spare it, and will not let it go,
But keep it still within his mouth;
Yet his meat in his bowels is turned,
It is the gall of asps within him.
He hath swallowed down riches, and he shall vomit them
        up again:
God shall cast them out of his belly.
He shall suck the poison of asps:
The viper's tongue shall slay him.
He shall not look upon the rivers,
The flowing streams of honey and butter.
That which he labored for shall he restore, and shall not
        swallow it down;
According to the substance that he hath gotten, he shall
        not rejoice.
For he hath oppressed and forsaken the poor;

He hath violently taken away an house, and he shall not
    build it up.
Because he knew no quietness within him,
He shall not save aught of that wherein he delighteth.
There was nothing left that he devoured not ;
Therefore his prosperity shall not endure.
In the fullness of his sufficiency he shall be in straits :
The hand of every one that is in misery shall come upon
    him.
When he is about to fill his belly,
God shall cast the fierceness of his wrath upon him,
And shall rain it upon him while he is eating.
He shall flee from the iron weapon,
And the bow of brass shall strike him through.
He draweth it forth, and it cometh out of his body :
Yea, the glittering point cometh out of his gall ;
Terrors are upon him.
All darkness is laid up for his treasures :
A fire not blown by man shall devour him ;
It shall consume that which is left in his tent.
The heavens shall reveal his iniquity,
And the earth shall rise up against him.
   The increase of his house shall depart,
His goods shall flow[1] away in the day of his wrath.
This is the portion of a wicked man from God,
And the heritage appointed unto him by God.

  Job.[2] Hear diligently my speech ;
And let this be your consolations!   [*With sarcasm.*
   Suffer me, and I also will speak ;
And after that I have spoken, mock on.

---

[1] For example, as thine have gone.
[2] "Then Job answered and said," etc.

I.

As for me, is my complaint to man?

II.

And why should I not be impatient?

[No answer.

Mark me, and be astonished,
And lay your hand upon your mouth.
[Job is troubled when he thinks of the prosperous wicked.
Even when I remember I am troubled,
And horror taketh hold on my flesh.
  Wherefore do the wicked live,
Become old, yea, wax mighty in power?
Their seed is established with them in their sight,
And their offspring before their eyes.
Their houses are safe from fear,
Neither is the rod of God upon them.
Their bull gendereth, and faileth not;
Their cow calveth, and casteth not her calf.
They send forth their little ones like a flock,
And their children dance.
They sing to the timbrel and harp,
And rejoice at the sound of the pipe.
They spend their days in prosperity,
And in a moment they go down to Sheol.
And they say unto God,
" Depart from us;
For we desire not the knowledge of thy ways.
What is the Almighty, that we should serve him?
And what profit should we have, if we pray unto him?"

Lo, their prosperity is not in their hand!   *[Ironically.*
[I say it is, though] The counsel of the wicked is far
    from me.

5

How oft is it that the lamp of the wicked is put out?
That their calamity cometh upon them?
That God distributeth sorrows in his anger?
That they are as stubble before the wind,
And as chaff that the storm carrieth away?

Ye [I] say,[1] God layeth up his iniquity for his children.
Let him recompense it unto himself,[2] that he may know it.
Let his own eyes see his destruction,
And let him drink of the wrath of the Almighty.
For what pleasure hath he[3] in his house after him,
When the number of his months is cut off?
[Ye ask.]   Shall any teach God knowledge?
Seeing he judgeth those that are high.
   [Yet!] One dieth in his full strength,
   Being wholly at ease and quiet:
   His breasts are full of milk,
   And the marrow of his bones is moistened.
   And another dieth in bitterness of soul,
   And never tasteth of good.
They lie down alike in the dust,
And the worm covereth them.

[Becomes personal.

Behold, I know your thoughts,
And the devices which ye wrongfully imagine against
     me.
For ye say,
" Where is the house of the prince?" and
" Where is the tent wherein the wicked dwelt?"
Have ye not asked them that go by the way?

---

[1] *Ye say* should be, *I say,* etc.
[2] That is, upon the offender that the offender may know, etc.
[3] The righteous.

And do ye not know their tokens?
That the evil man is reserved to the day of calamity?
That they are led forth to the day of wrath?

[*Job asks them.*] Who shall declare his way to his face?
And who shall repay him what [wickedness] he hath
    done?
Yet shall he be borne to the grave,
And men shall keep watch over the tomb.
The clods of the valley shall be sweet unto him,
And all men shall draw after him,
As there were innumerable before him.

How then comfort ye me in vain,
Seeing in your answers there remaineth only falsehood?
                           [*Exeunt.*

SCENE VIII. A Tent.

JOB within. Time, night.[1] Lamp burning.

Enter ELIPHAZ, BILDAD, ZOPHAR. They sit before the tent.

Eliphaz.[2] Can a man be profitable unto God?
Surely he that is wise is profitable unto himself.
Is it any pleasure to the Almighty, that thou art right-
    eous.   [*Sarcastically.*
Or is it gain to him, that thou makest thy ways perfect?
Is it for thy fear of him that he reproveth thee,
That he entereth with thee into judgment?
Is not thy wickedness great?   [*Directly accuses Job.*
Neither is there any end to thine iniquities.

---

[1] Time, night, xxii, 12; xxv, 5, moon and stars visible.
[2] " Then answered Eliphaz the Temanite, and said," etc.

For thou hast taken pledges of thy brother for nought,
And stripped the naked of their clothing.
Thou hast not given water to the weary to drink,
And thou hast withholden bread from the hungry.
But as for the mighty man, he had the earth;
And the honorable man, he dwelt in it.
Thou hast sent widows away empty,
And the arms of the fatherless have been broken.
Therefore snares are around about thee,
And sudden fear troubleth thee,
Or darkness, that thou canst not see,
And abundance of waters cover thee.

Is not God in the height of heaven?
And behold the height of the stars how high they are!
And thou sayest,
" What doth God know?
Can he judge through the thick darkness?
Thick clouds are a covering to him, that he seeth not;
And he walketh on the vault of heaven."
    Wilt thou keep the old way
Which wicked men have trodden?
Who were snatched away before their time,
Whose foundation was poured out as a stream:
Who said unto God,
" Depart from us;" and
" What can the Almighty do for us?"
Yet he filled their houses with good things: [Thou sayest.]
[And thou sayest also.]   " But the counsel of the wicked
        is far from me."[1]
[Not so.]   The righteous see it,[2] and are glad;
And the innocent laugh them to scorn: saying,

---

[1] See Act III, Scene VII, page 65.   [2] The destruction of the wicked.

" Surely they that did rise up against us are cut off,
And the remnant of them the fire hath consumed."

[Eliphaz once more inclined to kindness.

Acquaint now thyself with him, and be at peace :
Thereby good shall come unto thee.
Receive, I pray thee, the law from his mouth,
And lay up his words in thine heart.
(If thou return to the Almighty, thou shalt be built up ;
If thou put away unrighteousness far from thy tents.)
And lay thou thy treasure in the dust,
And the gold of Ophir among the stones of the brooks ;
And the Almighty shall be thy treasure,
And precious silver unto thee.
For then shalt thou delight thyself in the Almighty,
And lift up thy face unto God.
Thou shalt make thy prayer unto him, and he shall hear thee ;
And thou shalt pay thy vows.
Thou shalt also decree a thing, and it shall be established
       unto thee ;
And light shall shine upon thy ways.
When they cast thee down, thou shalt say,
" There is lifting up ; "
And the humble person he shall save.
He shall deliver even him that is not innocent :
Yea, he shall be delivered through the cleanness of thine
       hands.

[Job paces to and fro.

Job.[1] Even to-day is my complaint rebellious :
My stroke is heavier than my groaning.

[He longs to receive justice.

O that I knew where I might find him,
That I might come even to his seat !

---

[1] " Then Job answered and said," etc.

I would order my cause before him,
And fill my mouth with arguments.
I would know the words which he would answer me,
And understand what he would say unto me.
  Would he contend with me in the greatness of his
    power ?
Nay; but he would give heed unto me.
There[1] the upright might reason with him ;
So should I be delivered forever from my judge.

                                                [Laments.

Behold, I go forward, but he is not there ;
And backward, but I cannot perceive him :
On the left hand, when he doth work, but I cannot be-
    hold him :
He hideth himself on the right hand, that I cannot see
    him.

       [A ray of encouragement flashes across Job's mind.
But he knoweth the way that I take ;
When he hath tried me, I shall come forth as gold.
My foot hath held fast to his steps ;
His way have I kept, and turned not aside.
I have not gone back from the commandment of his
    lips ;
I have treasured up the words of his mouth more than my
    necessary food.

       [Considers the situation and is again discouraged.
But he is in one mind, and who can turn him ?
And what his soul desireth, even that he doeth.
For he performeth that which is appointed for me :
And many such things are with him.
Therefore am I troubled at his presence :

---

[1] At a judge's tribunal.

When I consider, I am afraid of him.
For God hath made my heart faint,
And the Almighty hath troubled me :
Because I was not cut off before the darkness,[1]
Neither did he cover the thick darkness from my face.

　　[Petulant, and again longs for a fair public tria
Why are times not laid up by the Almighty ?
And why do not they which know him see his days ?

*[Becomes accusative, and declares during the remainder
　　of this speech that the righteous have no advan-
　　tage over the wicked.*

There are that remove the landmarks ;
They violently take away flocks, and feed them.
They drive away the ass of the fatherless,
They take the widow's ox for a pledge.
　They turn the needy out of the way :
The poor of the earth all hide themselves.
Behold, as wild asses in the desert
They go forth to their work, seeking diligently for meat ;
The wilderness yieldeth them food for their children.
They cut their provender in the field ;
And they glean the vintage of the wicked [who oppress
　　them].
They lie all night naked, without clothing,
And have no covering in the cold.
They are wet with the showers of the mountains,
And embrace the rock for want of a shelter.

　　　　　　　　　　[Repeats emphatically.
There are that pluck the fatherless from the breast,
And take a pledge of the poor :
So that they go about naked without clothing,

---

[1] That is, before these afflictions came upon me.

And being hungry they carry the sheaves;
They make oil within the walls of these men;
They tread their wine-presses, and suffer thirst.
From out of the populous city [also] men groan,
And the soul of the wounded crieth out:
Yet God regardeth not the folly!
These are of them that rebel against the light;
They know not the ways thereof,
Nor abide in the paths thereof.
The murderer riseth with the light, he killeth the poor
    and needy;
And in the night he is as a thief.
The eye also of the adulterer waiteth for the twilight,
    saying,
"No eye shall see me:"
And he disguiseth his face.
    In the dark they dig through houses:
They shut themselves up in the day-time;
They know not the light.

[Ye say] For the morning is to all of them[1] as the shadow
    of death;
For they know the terrors of the shadow of death.
He [Death] is swift upon the face of the waters;
Their portion is cursed in the earth;
He turneth not by the way of the vineyards.
Drought and heat consume the snow waters:
So doth Sheol[2] those which have sinned.
The womb shall forget him; the worm shall sweetly feed
    on him;
He shall be no more remembered:
And unrighteousness shall be broken as a tree.

---

[1] The wicked.   [2] The grave.

[I say] He [Death] devoureth the barren that beareth not;
And doeth not good to the widow.
He draweth away the mighty also by his power:
He riseth up, and no man is sure of life.
    God giveth them[1] to be in security, and they rest
        thereon;
And his eyes are upon their ways.
They are exalted; yet a little while, and they are gone;
Yea, they are brought low, they are taken out of the way
        as all other,
And are cut off as the tops of the ears of corn.

[*Grows defiant and refers to his own case as one righteous
    who is being cut off as a sinner.*

And if it be not so now, who will prove me a liar,
And make my speech of nothing worth?

Bildad.[2] Dominion and fear are with him;
He maketh peace in his high places.
Is there any number of his armies?
And upon whom doth not his light arise?
How then can man be just with God?
Or how can he be clean that is born of a woman?
Behold, even the moon hath no brightness,
And the stars are not pure in his sight:
How much less man, that is a worm!
And the son of man, which is a worm!
                    [*With extreme contempt.*
    Job.[3] How hast thou helped him that is without
    power!

---

[1] The righteous.
[2] "Then answered Bildad the Shuhite, and said," etc.
[3] "Then Job answered and said," etc.

How hast thou saved the arm that hath no strength!
How hast thou counseled him that hath no wisdom,
And plentifully declared sound knowledge!
To whom hast thou uttered words?
And whose spirit cometh forth from thee?   [*Exeunt.*

SCENE IX. *An Isolated Spot: A Storm Passing on the Sea.*

Enter JOB.

Job. They that are deceased tremble
Beneath the waters and the inhabitants thereof.
Sheol is naked before him,
And Abaddon hath no covering.
He stretcheth out the north over empty space,
And hangeth the earth upon nothing.
He bindeth up the waters in his thick clouds;
And the cloud is not rent under them.
He closeth in the face of his throne,
And spreadeth his cloud upon it.
He hath described a boundary upon the face of the waters,
Unto the confines of light and darkness.
The pillars of heaven tremble
And are astonished at his rebuke.
He stirreth up the sea with his power,
And by his understanding he smiteth through Rahab.
By his spirit the heavens are garnished;

His hand hath pierced the swift serpent.
Lo, these are but the outskirts of his ways:
And how small a whisper do we hear of him!
But the thunder of his power who can understand?

[*Spoken in dejection.*

Enter ELIPHAZ, BILDAD, *and* ZOPHAR.

[*Job*[1] *turns upon them.*

As God liveth, who hath taken away my right;
And the Almighty, who hath vexed my soul;
  (For my life is yet whole in me,
And the spirit of God in my nostrils;)
Surely my lips shall not speak unrighteousness,
Neither shall my tongue utter deceit.

God forbid that I should justify you:
Till I die I will not put away mine integrity from me.

[*Repeats it emphatically.*

My righteousness I hold fast, and will not let it go:
My heart shall not reproach me so long as I live.

Let mine enemy be as the wicked,
And let him that riseth up against me be as the unright-
    eous.
For what is the hope of the godless, though he get him
    gain,
When God taketh away his soul?
Will God hear his cry,
When trouble cometh upon him?
Will he delight himself in the Almighty,
And call upon God at all times?

---

[1] "And Job again took up his parable, and said," etc.

I will teach you concerning the hand of God ;
That which is with the Almighty will I not conceal.
Behold, all ye yourselves have seen it ;
Why then are ye become altogether vain ?

[*Then Job suddenly determines to show that he thoroughly understands their arguments, and iron-
ically proceeds to recount them, as follows :*[1]

This is the portion of a wicked man with God,
And the heritage of oppressors, which they receive from
          the Almighty :
  If his children be multiplied, it is for the sword ;
And his offspring shall not be satisfied with bread.
Those that remain of him shall be buried in death,
And his widows shall make no lamentation.
  Though he heap up silver as the dust,
And prepare raiment as the clay ;
He may prepare it, but the just shall put it on,
And the innocent shall divide the silver.
  He buildeth his house as the moth,
And as a booth which the keeper maketh.
He lieth down rich, but he shall not be gathered ;
He openeth his eyes, and he is not.
  Terrors overtake him like waters ;
A tempest stealeth him away in the night.
The east wind carrieth him away, and he departeth ;
And it sweepeth him out of his place.
For God shall hurl at him, and not spare :
He would fain flee out of his hand.

---

[1] Some scholars claim that the next twenty-two lines are Zophar's speech ;
his name, they say, has been omitted by transcribers. I have not felt at liberty
to insert Zophar's name.—*A. W.*

Men shall clap their hands at him,
And shall hiss him out of his place.

[*Exeunt the Three Friends.*
[*Job's great soliloquy on Wisdom begins.*

Surely there is a mine for silver,
And a place for gold which they refine.
Iron is taken out of the earth,
And brass is molten out of the stone.
Man setteth an end to darkness,
And searcheth out to the furthest bound—
The stones of thick darkness and of the shadow of death.
He breaketh open a shaft away from where men sojourn.
   They [the waters] are forgotten of the foot;
They hang afar from men, they swing to and fro.
As for the earth, out of it cometh bread:
And underneath it is turned up as it were by fire.
The stones thereof are the place of sapphires,
And it hath dust of gold.
That path[1] no bird of prey knoweth,
Neither hath the falcon's eye seen it:
The proud beasts have not trodden it,
Nor hath the fierce lion passed thereby.
   He [man] putteth forth his hand upon the flinty rock;
He overturneth the mountains by the roots.
He cutteth out channels among the rocks;
And his eye seeth every precious thing.
He bindeth the streams that they trickle not;
And the thing that is hid bringeth he forth to light.
But where shall wisdom be found?
And where is the place of understanding?
   Man knoweth not the price thereof;
Neither is it found in the land of the living.

---

[1] *"There is a path,"* etc. (Authorized Version).

The deep saith, " It is not in me : "
And the sea saith, " It is not with me."
It cannot be gotten for gold,
Neither shall silver be weighed for the price thereof.
It cannot be valued with the gold of Ophir,
With the precious onyx, or the sapphire.
Gold and glass cannot equal it :
Neither shall it be exchanged for jewels of fine gold.
No mention shall be made of coral or of crystal :
Yea, the price of wisdom is above rubies.
The topaz of Ethiopia shall not equal it,
Neither shall it be valued with pure gold.
  Whence then cometh wisdom ?
And where is the place of understanding ?
Seeing it is hid from the eyes of all living,
And kept close from the fowls of the air.
Destruction and Death say,
" We have heard a rumor thereof with our ears."
  God understandeth the way thereof,
And he knoweth the place thereof.
For he looketh to the ends of the earth,
And seeth under the whole heaven ;
To make a weight for the wind ;
Yea, he meteth out the waters by measure.
When he made a decree for the rain,
And a way for the lightning of the thunder :
Then did he see it, and declare it ;
He established it, yea, and searched it out.
And unto man he said,
" Behold, the fear of the Lord, that is wisdom ;
And to depart from evil is understanding."   [*Exit.*

SCENE X.   *The Open Country.*

Enter JOB.

Job : [1] O that I were as in the months of old,
As in the days when God watched over me ;
When his lamp shined upon my head,
And by his light I walked through darkness ;
As I was in the ripeness of my days,
When the secret of God was upon my tent ;
When the Almighty was yet with me,
And my children were about me ;
When my steps were washed with butter, [2]
And the rock poured me out streams of oil !
When I went forth to the gate unto the city,
When I prepared my seat in the street,
The young men saw me and hid themselves,

---

[1] " And Job again took up his parable, and said," etc.
[2] Job thinks of the mammoth dairies he once had.

And the aged rose up and stood;
The princes refrained talking,
And laid their hand on their mouth;
The voice of the nobles was hushed,
And their tongue cleaved to the roof of their mouth.
For when the ear heard me, Then it blessed me;
And when the eye saw me, it gave witness unto me:
Because I delivered the poor that cried,
The fatherless also, that had none to help him.

The blessing of him that was ready to perish came upon
      me:
And I caused the widow's heart to sing for joy.
I put on righteousness, and it clothed me:
My justice was as a robe and a diadem.
I was eyes to the blind,
And feet was I to the lame.
I was a father to the needy:
And the cause of him that I knew not I searched out.
And I brake the jaws of the unrighteous,
And plucked the prey out of his teeth.

Then I said, I shall die in my nest,
And I shall multiply my days as the sand:
My root is spread out to the waters,
And the dew lieth all night upon my branch:
My glory is fresh in me,
And my bow is renewed in my hand.

Unto me men gave ear, and waited,
And kept silence for my counsel.
After my words they spake not again;
And my speech dropped upon them.
  6

And they waited for me as for the rain ;
And they opened their mouth wide as for the latter rain.
If I laughed on them, they believed it not ;
And the light of my countenance they cast not down.
I chose out their way, and sat as chief,
And dwelt as a king in the army,
As one that comforteth mourners.

[*The dark side of the contrast.*
But now they that are younger than I have me in derision,
Whose fathers I disdained to set with the dogs of my
    flock.
Yea, the strength of their hands, whereto should it profit
    me?
Men [fathers] in whom ripe age is perished.
    They [sons of such fathers] are gaunt with want and
        famine ;
They gnaw the dry ground, in the gloom of wasteness and
    desolation.
They pluck salt-wort by the bushes ;
And the roots of the broom are their meat.
They are driven forth from the midst of men ;
They [other men] cry after them as after a thief.
In the clefts of the valleys must they dwell,
In holes of the earth and of the rocks.
Among the bushes they bray ;
Under the nettles they are gathered together.
They are children of fools, yea, children of base men ;
They were scourged out of the land.
            [*Job proceeds in awful humiliation.*
And now I am become their song,
Yea, I am a by-word unto them.

They abhor me, they stand aloof from me,
And spare not to spit in my face.
For he hath loosed his cord, and afflicted me,
And they have cast off the bridle before me.
Upon my right hand rise the rabble;
They thrust aside my feet,
And they cast up against me their ways of destruction.
They mar my path,
They set forward my calamity,
Even men that have no helper.
As through a wide breach they come :
In the midst of the ruin they roll themselves upon me.
Terrors are turned upon me,
They chase mine honor as the wind;
And my welfare is passed away as the cloud.

      [He speaks of his physical distress.
And now my soul is poured out within me;
Days of affliction have taken hold upon me.
In the night season my bones are pierced in me,
And the pains that gnaw me take no rest.
By the great force of my disease is my garment dis-
  figured :
It bindeth me about as the collar of my coat.
He hath cast me in the mire,
And I am become like dust and ashes.

          [Prays.
" I cry unto thee, and thou dost not answer me :
I stand up, and thou lookest at me.
Thou art turned to be cruel to me :
With the might of thy hand thou persecutest me.
Thou liftest me up to the wind, thou causest me to ride
  upon it;
And thou dissolvest me in the storm.

For I know that thou wilt bring me to death,
And to the house appointed for all living."

> *[Continues his soliloquy hopefully.*

Surely against a ruinous heap he will not put forth his hand;

> *[Immediately becomes fretful.*

Though it be in his destruction, one may utter a cry because
of these things.

  Did not I weep for him that was in trouble?
Was not my soul grieved for the needy?

> *[Moans on in anguish.*

When I looked for good, then evil came;
And when I waited for light, there came darkness.

> *[Restlessly paces to and fro.*

My bowels boil, and rest not;
Days of affliction are come upon me.
I go mourning without the sun:
I stand up in the assembly, and cry for help.
I am a brother to jackals,
And a companion to ostriches.
My skin is black, and falleth from me,
And my bones are burned with heat!
Therefore is my harp turned to mourning,
And my pipe into the voice of them that weep.

> *[Quiet reigns; then Job, wondering at the cause of his
> fate, recounts possible evils for which punishment
> could come.*

> *[He is not guilty of fornication.*

I made a covenant with mine eyes;
How then should I look upon a maid?
For what is the portion from God above,
And the heritage from the Almighty on high?
Is it not calamity to the unrighteous,
And disaster to the workers of iniquity?

[Asserts his integrity.

Doth not he see my ways,
And number all my steps ?
If I have walked with vanity,
And my foot hath hasted to deceit ;
(Let me be weighed in an even balance,
That God may know mine integrity ;)
If my step hath turned out of the way,
And mine heart walked after mine eyes,
And if any spot hath cleaved to mine hands :
Then let me sow, and let another eat ;
Yea, let the produce of my field be rooted out.

[Not guilty of adultery.

If mine heart have been enticed unto a woman,
And I have laid wait at my neighbor's door :
Then let my wife grind unto another,
And let others bow down upon her.
For that were an heinous crime ;
Yea, it were an iniquity to be punished by the judges :
For it is a fire that consumeth unto Destruction,
And would root out all mine increase.

[Nor has he been unjust to his servants.

If I did despise the cause of my man-servant or of my
    maid-servant,
When they contended with me :
What then shall I do when God riseth up ?
And when he visiteth, what shall I answer him ?
Did not he that made me in the womb make him ?
And did not one fashion us in the womb ?

[Nor neglectful of the poor.

If I have withheld the poor from their desire,
Or have caused the eyes of the widow to fail ;
Or have eaten my morsel alone,

And the fatherless hath not eaten thereof;
(Nay, from my youth he grew up with me as with a father,
And her have I guided from my mother's womb;)
If I have seen any perish for want of clothing,
Or that the needy had no covering;
If his loins have not blessed me,
And if he were not warmed with the fleece of my sheep;
If I have lifted up my hand against the fatherless,
Because I saw my help in the gate:
Then let my shoulder fall from the shoulder-blade,
And mine arm be broken from the bone.
For calamity from God was a terror to me,
And by reason of his majesty I could do nothing.

    [Neither miserly, nor an idolater.

If I have made gold my hope,
And have said to the fine gold, "Thou art my confi-
  dence;"
If I rejoiced because my wealth was great,
And because mine hand had gotten much;
If I beheld the sun when it shined,
Or the moon walking in brightness;
And my heart hath been secretly enticed,
And my mouth hath kissed my hand:[1]
This also were an iniquity to be punished by the judges:
For I should have lied to God that is above.

    [Nor did he rejoice over enemies.

If I rejoiced at the destruction of him that hated me,
Or lifted up myself when evil found him;
Yea, I suffered not my mouth to sin
By asking his life with a curse;

---

[1] The worship of the heavenly bodies was the oldest and also the purest form of idolatry. Kissing the hand, or throwing a kiss by the hand, was one of the forms which the worship took.—*Thornley Smith.*

[Not inhospitable.

If the men of my tent said not,
" Who can find one that hath not been filled with his meat ? "
The stranger did not lodge in the street;
But I opened my doors to the traveler;

[Did not fear the people.

If like Adam I covered my transgressions,
By hiding iniquity in my bosom;
Because I feared the great multitude,
And the contempt of families terrified me,
So that I kept silence, and went not out of the door:
[Here Job breaks off his retrospect and exclaims with honest pride and longing:
O that I had one to hear me!
(Lo, here is my signature, [that is, my innocence!] let [even]
    the Almighty answer me;)
And that I had the indictment which mine adversary hath
    written!
Surely I would carry it upon my shoulder;
I would bind it unto me as a crown.
I would declare unto him the number of my steps;
As a prince would I go near unto him.
*[Since Job has never injured man he calls upon the very
    earth itself to punish him if he has wronged it.*
If my land cry out against me,
And the furrows thereof weep together;
If I have eaten the fruits thereof without money,
Or have caused the owners thereof to lose their life:
Let thistles grow instead of wheat,
And cockle instead of barley.   *[Exit.*[1]

---

[1] " The words of Job are ended.
" So [also] these three men ceased to answer Job, because he was righteous in his own eyes."

PROLOGUE TO ACT IV.

Then was kindled the wrath of Elihu the son of Barachel
the Buzite, of the family of Ram :

I.

Against Job was his wrath kindled, because he justified
himself rather than God.

II.

Also against his three friends was his wrath kindled, because they had found no answer, and yet had condemned Job.

Now Elihu had waited to speak unto Job, because they
were elder than he.

And when Elihu saw that there was no answer in the
mouth of these three men, his wrath was kindled.

And Elihu the son of Barachel the Buzite answered and
said : (*See Act IV, Scene I, line* 1.)

ACT IV.

SCENE I.   *An Open Tent.*

JOB *within.*

Enter ELIHU, *expostulating with the Three Friends.*

Elihu.   I am young, and ye are very old ;
Wherefore I held back, and durst not show you mine
    opinion.
I said, " Days should speak,
And multitude of years should teach wisdom."
But there is a spirit in man,
And the breath of the Almighty giveth them understand-
    ing.
It is not the great that are wise,
Nor the aged that understand judgment.
Therefore I said, " Hearken to me ;
I also will show mine opinion."

Behold, I waited for your words,
I listened for your reasons,
Whilst ye searched out what to say.
Yea, I attended unto you,
And, behold, there was none that convinced Job,
Or that answered his words, among you.
Beware lest ye say, " We have found wisdom ; "
God may vanquish him, not man :
For he hath not directed his words against me ;
Neither will I answer him with your speeches.

                    [*Approaches Job and soliloquizes.*
They are amazed, they answer no more :
They have not a word to say.
And shall I wait, because they speak not,
Because they stand still, and answer no more ?
    I also will answer my part,
I also will show mine opinion.
For I am full of words ;
The spirit within me constraineth me.
Behold, my breast is as wine which hath no vent ;
Like new bottles it is ready to burst.
I will speak, that I may be refreshed ;
I will open my lips and answer.

[*To Job.*] Let me not, I pray you, respect any man's person ;
Neither will I give flattering titles to any man.
For I know not to give flattering titles ;
Else would my Maker soon take me away.
Howbeit, Job, I pray thee, hear my speech,
And hearken to all my words.
Behold, now [that] I have opened my mouth,
[That] my tongue hath spoken in my mouth,
My words shall utter the uprightness of my heart :

And that which my lips know they shall speak sincerely.
  The spirit of God hath made me,
And the breath of the Almighty giveth me life.
If thou canst, answer thou me;
Set thy words in order before me, stand forth.
Behold, I am toward God even as thou art:
I also am formed out of the clay.
Behold, my terror shall not make thee afraid,
Neither shall my pressure be heavy upon thee.

          [*Begins his opposition by citing Job's own words.*
Surely thou hast spoken in mine hearing,
And I have heard the voice of thy words, saying,

First Statement.

" I am clean, without transgression;
I am innocent, neither is there iniquity in me:
Behold, he findeth occasions against me,
He counteth me for his enemy;
He putteth my feet in the stocks,
He marketh all my paths."

First Argument.

Behold, I will answer thee, in this thou art not just:
For God is greater than man.
Why dost thou strive against him?
For he giveth not account of any of his matters.
          [*Yet Elihu shows that God does two things.*
For God speaketh once,
Yea twice, though man regardeth it not.

I.

In a dream, in a vision of the night,
When deep sleep falleth upon men,

In slumberings upon the bed;
Then he openeth the ears of men,
And sealeth their instruction,
That he may withdraw man from his purpose,
And hide pride from man;
He keepeth back his soul from the pit,
And his life from perishing by the sword.

II.

He is chastened also with pain upon his bed, [*as thou art*,]
And with continual strife in his bones:
So that his life abhorreth bread,
And his soul dainty meat.
His flesh is consumed away, that it cannot be seen;
And his bones that were not seen stick out, [as do thine.]
Yea, his soul draweth near unto the pit,
And his life to the destroyers.
  If there be with him an angel,
An interpreter, one among a thousand,
To show unto man what is right for him;
Then he is gracious unto him, and saith,
"Deliver him from going down to the pit,
I have found a ransom."
  His flesh shall be fresher than a child's;
He returneth to the days of his youth:
He prayeth unto God, and he is favorable unto him;
So that he seeth his face with joy:
And he restoreth unto man his righteousness.
He singeth before men, and saith,
"I have sinned, and perverted that which was right,
And it profited me not:
He hath redeemed my soul from going into the pit,
And my life shall behold the light."

Lo, all these things doth God work,
Twice, yea thrice, with a man,
To bring back his soul from the pit,
That he may be enlightened with the light of the living.

PREFACE TO SECOND STATEMENT AND ARGUMENT.

Mark well, O Job, hearken unto me :
Hold thy peace, and I will speak.
If thou hast any thing to say, answer me :
Speak, for I desire to justify thee.
If not, hearken thou unto me :
Hold thy peace, and I will teach thee wisdom.

[*Job will not speak, and Elihu*[1] *again addresses the Three Friends.*

Hear my words, ye wise men ;
And give ear unto me, ye that have knowledge.
For the ear trieth words,
As the palate tasteth meat.
Let us choose for us that which is right :
Let us know among ourselves what is good.
For Job hath said :

SECOND STATEMENT.

" I am righteous,
And God hath taken away my right :
Notwithstanding my right I am accounted a liar ;
My wound is incurable, though I am without transgression."
What man is like Job,
Who drinketh up scorning like water ?

---

[1] " Moreover Elihu answered and said," etc.

Which goeth in company with the workers of iniquity,
And walketh with wicked men.
For he hath said,
" It profiteth a man nothing
That he should delight himself with God."

Second Argument.

I. (*To the Three.*)

Therefore hearken unto me, ye men of understanding :
Far be it from God, that he should do wickedness ;
And from the Almighty, that he should commit iniquity.
For the work of a man shall he render unto him,
And cause every man to find according to his ways.
Yea, of a surety, God will not do wickedly,
Neither will the Almighty pervert judgment.
Who gave him a charge over the earth ?
Or who hath disposed the whole world ?
If he set his heart upon man,
If he gather unto himself his spirit and his breath ;
All flesh shall perish together,
And man shall turn again unto dust.

II. (*To Job.*)

If now thou hast understanding, hear this :
Hearken to the voice of my words.
Shall even one that hateth right govern ?
And wilt thou condemn him that is just and mighty ?
Is it fit to say to a king, "Thou art vile ? "
Or to nobles, " Ye are wicked ? "
How much less to him that respecteth not the persons of
        princes,
Nor regardeth the rich more than the poor ?
For they are all the work of his hands.

In a moment they die, even at midnight;
The people are shaken and pass away,
And the mighty are taken away without hand.
For his eyes are upon the ways of a man,
And he seeth all his goings.
There is no darkness, nor shadow of death,
Where the workers of iniquity may hide themselves.
For he needeth not further to consider a man,
That he should go before God in judgment.
   He breaketh in pieces mighty men in ways past finding
     out,
And setteth others in their stead.
Therefore he taketh knowledge of their works;
And he overturneth them in the night, so that they are
     destroyed.
He striketh them as wicked men
In the open sight of others;
Because they turned aside from following him,
And would not have regard to any of his ways:
So that they caused the cry of the poor to come unto him,
And he heard the cry of the afflicted.
   He giveth quietness, who then can condemn him?
And when he hideth his face, who then can behold him?
Alike whether it be done unto a nation, or unto a man:
That the godless man reign not,
That there be none to ensnare the people.
For hath any said unto God,
" I have borne chastisement, I will not offend any more:
That which I see not teach thou me:
If I have done iniquity, I will do it no more!"
Shall his recompense be as thou wilt, that thou refusest it?
For thou [Job] must choose, and not I:
Therefore speak what thou knowest.

[*Job does not deign to notice Elihu ; so, exasperated, he drops the argument and turns to the* **Three**.

Men of understanding will say unto me,
Yea, every wise man that heareth me :
Job speaketh without knowledge,
And his words are without wisdom.
  Would that Job were tried unto the end,
Because of his answering like wicked men.
For he addeth rebellion unto his sin,
He clappeth his hands among us,
And multiplieth his words against God.

THIRD STATEMENT.[1]

[*To Job.*] Thinkest thou this to be thy right,
Or sayest thou, " My righteousness is more than God's,"
That thou sayest, " What advantage will it be unto thee ? "
And, " What profit shall I have more than if I had sinned ? "
I will answer thee,
And thy companions with thee.[2]

THIRD ARGUMENT.

  Look unto the heavens, and see;
And behold the skies, which are higher than thou.
If thou hast sinned, what effectest thou against him ?
And if thy transgressions be multiplied, what doest thou
    unto him ?
If thou be righteous, what givest thou him ?
Or what receiveth he of thine hand ?
Thy wickedness may hurt a man as thou art;

---

[1] " Moreover Elihu answered and said," etc.

[2] Elihu had not secured much sympathy from the Three in his appeal to them a few moments before.

And thy righteousness may profit a son of man.
By reason of the multitude of oppressions they [sons of
    -   men] cry out;
They cry for help by reason of the arm of the mighty.
But none saith,
" Where is God my Maker,
Who giveth songs in the night;
Who teacheth us more than the beasts of the earth,
And maketh us wiser than the fowls of heaven ?"
There they cry, but none giveth answer,
Because of the pride of evil men.
    Surely God will not hear vanity,
Neither will the Almighty regard it.
How much less when thou sayest thou beholdest him not,
The cause is before him, and thou waitest for him !

[*Turns away from Job contemptuously and addresses the
    Friends.*

But now, because he hath not visited in his anger,
Neither doth he greatly regard arrogance ;
Therefore doth Job open his mouth in vanity;
He multiplieth words without knowledge.
        [*Exeunt Eliphaz, Bildad, Zophar, and Elihu.*
  7

SCENE II.   *A Covered Place.*

Time, night.   Lamp burning.

Enter JOB, *followed anon by* ELIHU.

Elihu.[1]   [*To Job.*]   Suffer me a little, and I will show
    thee;
For I have yet somewhat to say on God's behalf.
I will fetch my knowledge from afar,
And will ascribe righteousness to my Maker.
For truly my words are not false:
One that is perfect[2] in knowledge is with thee.

---

[1] " Elihu also proceeded, and said," etc.
[2] That is, one who knows what he is about when he speaks on this subject.

Fourth Argument.

Behold, God is mighty, and despiseth not any :
He is mighty in strength of understanding.
He preserveth not the life of the wicked :
But giveth to the afflicted their right.
He withdraweth not his eyes from the righteous :
But with kings upon the throne
He setteth them forever, and they are exalted.
And if they be bound in fetters,
And be taken in the cords of affliction ;
Then he showeth them their work,
And their transgressions, that they have behaved them-
    selves proudly.
He openeth also their ear to instruction,
And commandeth that they return from iniquity.
If they hearken and serve him,
They shall spend their days in prosperity,
And their years in pleasures.
But if they hearken not, they shall perish by the sword,
And they shall die without knowledge.
But [if] they that are godless in heart lay up anger :
They cry not for help when he bindeth them.
They die in youth,
And their life perisheth among the unclean.
  He delivereth the afflicted by his affliction,
And openeth their ear in oppression.
Yea, he would have led thee away out of distress
Into a broad place, where there is no straitness ;
And that which is set on thy table shall be full of fatness.

    [Elihu now despairs of moving impenitent Job.

But thou art full of the judgment of the wicked :
Judgment and justice take hold on thee !   *[Angrily.*

[*Job moves impatiently, and Elihu hastens to say.*

For let not wrath stir thee up against chastisements;
Neither let the greatness of the ransom turn thee aside.
Will thy riches suffice, that thou be not in distress,
Or all the forces of thy strength?

[*Elihu proceeds to warn him.*

Desire not the night,
When peoples are cut off in their place.
Take heed, regard not iniquity:
For this hast thou chosen rather than affliction.
Behold, God doeth loftily in his power:
Who is a teacher like unto him?
Who hath enjoined him his way?
Or who can say,
" Thou hast wrought unrighteousness?"
    Remember that thou magnify his work, whereof men
        have sung.
All men have looked thereon;
Man beholdeth it afar off.

Behold, God is great, and we know him not;
The number of his years is unsearchable.

[*Heavy rain.*

For he draweth up the drops of water,
Which distill in rain from his vapor:
Which the skies pour[1] down
And drop upon man abundantly.
Yea, can any understand the spreadings of the clouds?
The thunderings of his pavilion!
Behold, he spreadeth his light around him;   [*Lightning.*
And he covereth the bottom of the sea.

---

[1] Literally, " are pouring down."

For by these he judgeth the peoples ;
He giveth meat in abundance.
He covereth his hands with the lightning ;
And giveth it a charge that it strike the mark. [*Storming.*
The noise thereof telleth concerning him,
The cattle also concerning the storm that cometh up.

                   [*Great storming; Elihu is frightened.*
Yea, at this my heart trembleth,
And is moved out of its place.   [*Storming.*
Hear, O hear the noise of his voice,
And the sound that goeth out of his mouth.

                          [*Elihu excitedly.*
He sendeth it forth under the whole heaven,
And his lightning unto the ends of the earth.
After it a voice roareth ;   [*Continuous flash and roar.*
He thundereth with the voice of his majesty :
And he stayeth them not when his voice is heard.
[*Elihu in a lull of the storm, which is now evidently
      nearing its height, philosophizes.*
God thundereth marvelously with his voice ;
Great things doeth he, which we cannot comprehend.
For he saith to the snow, " Fall thou on the earth ; "
Likewise to the shower of rain,
And to the showers of his mighty rain.
He sealeth up the hand of every man ;
That all men whom he hath made may know it.
Then the beasts go into coverts,
And remain in their dens.
Out of the chamber of the south cometh the storm :
And cold out of the north.
By the breath of God ice is given :
And the breadth of the waters is straitened.
Yea, he ladeth the thick cloud with moisture ;

He spreadeth abroad the cloud of his lightning:
And it is turned round about by his guidance,
That they may do whatsoever he commandeth them
Upon the face of the habitable world:
Whether it be for correction, or for his land,
Or for mercy, that he cause it to come. [*The storm rages.*
Hearken unto this, O Job!
Stand still, and consider the wondrous works of God.
Dost thou know how God layeth his charge upon them,
And causeth the lightning of his cloud to shine?
Dost thou know the balancings of the clouds,
The wondrous works of him which is perfect in knowledge?
How thy garments are warm,
When the earth is still by reason of the south wind?

                      [*Fierce lightning.*
Canst thou with him spread out the sky,
Which is strong as a molten mirror?

    [*The lightnings leave intense darkness over the scene.*
Teach us what we shall say unto him [now];
For we cannot order our speech by reason of darkness.
Shall it be told him that I would speak?
Or should a man wish that he were swallowed up?

      [*A long pause while the storm is passing away.*
And now men see not the light which is bright in the skies:
But the wind passeth, and cleareth them.
Out of the north cometh golden splendor:
God hath upon him terrible majesty.

      [*Elihu now turns to Job with this conclusion.*
Touching the Almighty, we cannot find him out; he is
     excellent in power:
And in judgment and plenteous justice he will not afflict.
Men do therefore fear him:
He regardeth not any that are wise of heart.   [*Exeunt.*

ACT V.

SCENE I. *A Covered Place. Dawn. The Lord in a*
Whirlwind.

Enter JOB.

The Lord.[1] Who is this that darkeneth counsel
By words without knowledge?
Gird up now thy loins like a man;
For I will demand of thee, and declare thou unto me.

FIRST SERIES OF QUESTIONS: INANIMATE CREATION.

Where wast thou when I laid the foundations of the earth?
Declare, if thou hast understanding.   [*No answer.*
Who determined the measures thereof, if thou knowest?
Or who stretched the line upon it?
Whereupon were the foundations thereof fastened?
Or who laid the corner-stone thereof;
When the morning stars sang together,
And all the sons of God shouted for joy?
                              [*Silence, then a whirlwind.*

---

[1] "Then the Lord answered Job out of the whirlwind, and said," etc.

Or who shut up the sea with doors,
When it brake forth, as if it had issued out of the womb;
When I made the cloud the garment thereof,
And thick darkness a swaddling-band for it,
And marked out for it my bound,
And set bars and doors,
And said, "Hitherto shalt thou come, but no further;
And here shall thy proud waves be stayed?"

          [Silence, and whirlwind.

Hast thou commanded the morning since thy days began,
And caused the dayspring to know its place;
That it might take hold of the ends of the earth,
And the wicked be shaken out of it?
It is changed as clay under the seal;
And all things stand forth as a garment:
And from the wicked their light is withholden,
And the high arm is broken. *[Silence, and whirlwind.*

 Hast thou entered into the springs of the sea?
Or hast thou walked in the recesses of the deep?
Have the gates of death been revealed unto thee?
Or hast thou seen the gates of the shadow of death?
Hast thou comprehended the earth in its breadth?
Declare, if thou knowest it all.   *[No reply.*
Where is the way to the dwelling of light,
And as for darkness, where is the place thereof;
That thou shouldest take it to the bound thereof,
And that thou shouldest discern the paths to the house
  thereof?
Doubtless, thou knowest, for thou wast then born,
And the number of thy days is great!

          [Silence, and whirlwind.

Hast thou entered the treasuries of the snow,
Or hast thou seen the treasuries of the hail,

Which I have reserved against the time of trouble,
Against the day of battle and war?

> *[Pause, and whirlwind.*

By what way is the light parted,
Or the east wind scattered upon the earth?
Who hath cleft a channel for the water-flood,
Or a way for the lightning of the thunder;
To cause it to rain on a land where no man is;
On the wilderness, wherein there is no man;
To satisfy the waste and desolate ground;
And to cause the tender grass to spring forth?
  Hath the rain a father?
Or who hath begotten the drops of dew?
Out of whose womb came the ice?
And the hoary frost of heaven, who hath gendered it?
The waters hide themselves and become like stone,
And the face of the deep is frozen.

> *[Pause, and whirlwind.*

Canst thou bind the cluster of the Pleiades,
Or loose the bands of Orion?
Canst thou lead forth the Mazzaroth in their season?
Or canst thou guide the Bear with her train?
Knowest thou the ordinances of the heavens?
Canst thou establish the dominion thereof in the earth?
Canst thou lift up thy voice to the clouds,
That abundance of waters may cover thee?
Canst thou send forth lightnings, that they may go,
And say unto thee, "Here we are?"

[Job, perhaps thinking of the great storm, is silent still.
    See Act IV, Scene II.

Who hath put wisdom in the dark clouds?[1]
Or who hath given understanding to the meteor?[1]

---

[1] Marginal readings.

[*Whirlwind.*

Who can number the clouds by wisdom ?
Or who can pour out the bottles of heaven,
When the dust runneth into a mass,
And the clods cleave fast together ?

SECOND SERIES OF QUESTIONS : THE ANIMAL CREATION.

Wilt thou hunt the prey for the lioness ?
Or satisfy the appetite of the young lions,
When they crouch in their dens,
And abide in the covert to lie in wait ?

[*Pause, and whirlwind.*

Who provideth for the raven his prey,
When his young ones cry unto God,
And wander for lack of meat ?   [*Pause, and whirlwind.*
   Knowest thou the time when the wild goats of the rock
      bring forth ?
Or canst thou mark when the hinds do calve ?
Canst thou number the months that they fulfill ?
Or knowest thou the time when they bring forth ?
They bow themselves, they bring forth their young,
They cast out their sorrows.
Their young ones are in good liking, they grow up in the
      open field ;
They go forth, and return not again.

[*Pause, and whirlwind.*

Who hath sent out the wild ass free ?
Or who hath loosed the bands of the swift ass ?[1]

---

[1] Xenophon, speaking of the march through Arabia, wrote: "There were wild animals, however, of various kinds ; the most numerous were wild asses. There were also many ostriches, as well as bustards and antelopes ; and these animals the horsemen of the army sometimes hunted. The wild asses, when any one pursued them, would start forward a considerable distance, and then stand still (for they run much more swiftly than the horse) ; and again when

Whose house I have made the wilderness,
And the salt land his dwelling-place.
He scorneth the tumult of the city,
Neither heareth he the shoutings of the driver.
The range of the mountains is his pasture,
And he searcheth after every green thing.

                             [Pause, and whirlwind.

Will the wild ox be content to serve thee?
Or will he abide by thy crib?
Canst thou bind the wild ox with his band in the fur-
    row?
Or will he harrow the valleys after thee?
Wilt thou trust him, because his strength is great?
Or wilt thou leave to him thy labor?
Wilt thou confide in him, that he will bring home thy
    seed,
And gather the corn of thy threshing-floor?

                             [Pause, and whirlwind.

The wings of the ostrich wave proudly;
But are they the pinions and plumage of love?
For she leaveth her eggs on the earth,
And warmeth them in the dust,
And forgetteth that the foot may crush them,
Or that the wild beast may trample them.
She dealeth hardly with her young ones, as if they were
    not hers:
Though her labor be in vain, she is without fear;
Because God hath deprived her of wisdom,
Neither hath he imparted to her understanding.

---

the horse approached they did the same; and it was impossible to catch them,
unless the horsemen, stationing themselves at intervals, kept up the pursuit
with a succession of horses. The flesh of those that were taken resembled
venison, but was more tender."—*Anabasis.*

What time she lifteth up herself on high,
She scorneth the horse and his rider.[1]

[Pause, and whirlwind.

Hast thou given the horse his might?
Hast thou clothed his neck with the quivering mane?
Hast thou made him leap as a locust?
The glory of his snorting is terrible.
He paweth in the valley, and rejoiceth in his strength :
He goeth out to meet the armed men.
He mocketh at fear, and is not dismayed ;
Neither turneth he back from the sword.
The quiver rattleth against him,
The flashing spear and the javelin.
He swalloweth the ground with fierceness and rage ;
Neither believeth he that it is the voice of the trumpet.
As oft as the trumpet soundeth he saith, Aha !
And he smelleth the battle afar off,
The thunder of the captains, and the shouting.

[Pause, and whirlwind.

Doth the hawk soar by thy wisdom,
And stretch her wings toward the south ?
   Doth the eagle mount up at thy command,
And make her nest on high ?
On the cliff she dwelleth and maketh her home,
Upon the point of the cliff, and the stronghold.
From thence she spieth out the prey ;
Her eyes behold it afar off.
Her young ones also suck up blood :
And where the slain are, there is she.

---

[1] "An ostrich no one succeeded in catching ; and those horsemen who hunted that bird soon desisted from the pursuit ; for it far outstripped them in its flight, using its feet for running, and its wings, raising them like a sail."—*Anabasis.*

Shall[1] he that cavileth contend with the Almighty?
He that argueth with God, let him answer it.

[God awaits Job's answer.

Job.[2] Behold, I am of small account; what shall I an-
swer thee?
I lay my hand upon my mouth.
Once have I spoken, and I will not answer;
Yea twice, but I will proceed no further. *[End of Scene I.*

---

[1] " Moreover the Lord answered Job, and said," etc.
[2] " Then Job answered the Lord, and said," etc.

SCENE II. *As before.   Later.   The Lord in a Whirl-wind.*

JOB *Alone.*

The Lord. [1] Gird up thy loins now like a man:
I will demand of thee, and declare thou unto me.

[*Job arises.*

Wilt thou even disannul my judgment?
Wilt thou condemn me, that thou mayest be justified?
Or hast thou an arm like God?
And canst thou thunder with a voice like him?

[*No answer.*

Deck thyself now with excellency and dignity;
And array thyself with honor and majesty.
Pour forth the overflowings of thine anger:
And look upon every one that is proud, and abase him.
Look upon every one that is proud, and bring him low;
And tread down the wicked where they stand.
Hide them in the dust together;

---

[1] " Then the Lord answered Job out of the whirlwind, and said," etc.

Bind their faces in the hidden place.
Then will I also confess of thee
That thine own right hand can save thee.

SECOND SERIES CONTINUED:[1]   ANIMAL CREATION.

Behold now behemoth,[2] which I made as well as thee;
He eateth grass as an ox.
Lo now, his strength is in his loins,
And his force is in the muscles of his belly.
He moveth his tail like a cedar:
The sinews of his thighs are knit together.
His bones are as tubes of brass;
His limbs are like bars of iron.
He is chief of the ways of God :
He only that made him giveth him his sword.
   Surely the mountains bring him forth food ;
Where all the beasts of the field do play.
He lieth under the lotus-trees,
In the covert of the reed, and the fen.
The lotus-trees cover him with their shadow ;
The willows of the brook compass him about.
   Behold, if a river overflow, he trembleth not :
He is confident, though Jordan swell even to his mouth.
Shall any take him when he is on the watch,
Or pierce through his nose with a snare ?
                         [*Silence, and whirlwind.*
Canst thou draw out leviathan [3] with a fish-hook ?
Or press down his tongue with a cord ?
Canst thou put a rope into his nose?
Or pierce his jaw through with a hook ?
Will he make many supplications unto thee ?

---

[1] See Act V, Scene 1.   [2] The hippopotamus.   [3] The crocodile.

Or will he speak soft words unto thee?
Will he make a covenant with thee,
That thou shouldest take him for a servant forever?
Wilt thou play with him as with a bird?
Or wilt thou bind him for thy maidens?
Shall the bands of fishermen make traffic of him?
Shall they part him among the merchants?
Canst thou fill his skin with barbed irons,
Or his head with fish-spears?
Lay thine hand upon him;
Remember the battle, and do so no more.·

    Behold, the hope of him is in vain:
Shall not one be cast down even at the sight of him?
None is so fierce that he dare stir him up:
Who then is he that can stand before me?
Who hath first given unto me, that I should repay
    him?
Whatsoever is under the whole heaven is mine.

                    [Job does not answer.

I will not keep silence concerning his limbs,
Nor his mighty strength, nor his goodly frame.
    Who can strip off his outer garment?
Who shall come within his double bridle?
Who can open the doors of his face?
Round about his teeth is terror.
His strong scales are his pride,
Shut up together as with a close seal.
One is so near to another,
That no air can come between them.
They are joined one to another;
They stick together, that they cannot be sundered.
    His sneezings flash forth light,

And his eyes are like the eyelids of the morning.
Out of his mouth go burning torches,
And sparks of fire leap forth.
Out of his nostrils a smoke goeth,
As of a seething pot and burning rushes.
His breath kindleth coals,
And a flame goeth forth from his mouth.
    In his neck abideth strength,
And terror danceth before him.
The flakes of his flesh are joined together :
They are firm upon him ; they cannot be moved.
His heart is as firm as a stone ;
Yea, firm as the nether millstone.
    When he raiseth himself up, the mighty are afraid :
By reason of consternation they are beside themselves.
If one lay at him with the sword, it cannot avail ;
Nor the spear, the dart, nor the pointed shaft.
He counteth iron as straw,
And brass as rotten wood.
The arrow cannot make him flee :
Slingstones are turned with him into stubble.
Clubs are counted as stubble :
He laugheth at the rushing of the javelin.
    His underparts are like sharp potsherds :
He spreadeth as it were a threshing wain upon the mire.
He maketh the deep to boil like a pot :
He maketh the sea like ointment.
He maketh a path to shine after him ;
One would think the deep to be hoary.
    Upon earth there is not his like,
That is made without fear.
He beholdeth every thing that is high :
He is king over all the sons of pride.
  8

Job. [1] I know that thou canst do all things,
And that no purpose of thine can be restrained.
Who [2] is this that hideth counsel without knowledge?
Therefore have I uttered that which I understood not,
Things too wonderful for me, which I knew not.
    Hear, I beseech thee, and I will speak ;
I will demand of thee, and declare thou unto me.
I had heard of thee by the hearing of the ear ;
But now mine eye seeth thee,
Wherefore I abhor myself, and repent
In dust and ashes.

[Job prostrates himself.
[Exit Job.

---

[1] " Then Job answered the Lord, and said," etc.
[2] As much as to say, Ah truly !   Who is this, etc.

SCENE III. *The Open Country.*

Enter ELIPHAZ.

The Lord. [1] My wrath is kindled against thee,
And against thy two friends:
For ye have not spoken of me the thing
That is right, as my servant Job hath.
    Now therefore, take unto you
Seven bullocks and seven rams,
And go to my servant Job,
And offer for yourselves a burnt-offering;
And my servant Job shall pray for you;
For him will I accept, that

---

[1] "And it was so, that after the Lord had spoken these words unto Job [*see Act V, Scenes* I *and* II] the Lord said to Eliphaz the Temanite," etc.

I deal with you not after your folly;
For ye have not spoken of me the thing
That is right, as my servant Job hath.

[*Exit Eliphaz.*

Postlogue.

So Eliphaz the Temanite and Bildad the Shuhite and
Zophar the Naamathite went, and did according as the
Lord commanded them.

And the Lord turned the captivity of Job, when he
prayed for his friends: and the Lord gave Job twice as
much as he had before.

Scene IV.   *Job's Dining Room.*

Brethren, Sisters, and Acquaintance.

Then came there unto him all his brethren, and all his
sisters, and all they that had been of his acquaintance before, and did eat bread with him in his house: and they
bemoaned him, and comforted him concerning all the evil
that the Lord had brought upon him: every man also gave
him a piece of money, and every one a ring of gold.

[*End of Act V.*

EPILOGUE.

So the Lord blessed the latter end of Job more than his beginning: and he had fourteen thousand sheep, and six thousand camels, and a thousand yoke of oxen, and a thousand she-asses.

He had also seven sons and three daughters. And he called the name of the first, Jemima; and the name of the second, Keziah; and the name of the third, Keren-happuch. And in all the land were no women found so fair as the daughters of Job: and their father gave them inheritance among their brethren.

And after this Job lived an hundred and forty years, and saw his sons and his sons' sons, even four generations. So Job died, being old and full of days.

APPENDIX⁻ I.

TEXTUAL CHANGES.

The following readings, suggested by the American Old Testament Revision Company, have been adopted in this edition, displacing the readings of the English Company. Both are here given for comparison.

I.   1 For "eschewed" read "turned away from"
     6 For "there was a day . . . and Satan" read "it came to pass on the day when . . . that Satan" So in ii, 1.
     8 For "escheweth" read "turneth away from" So in ii, 3.
   22 For "with foolishness" read "foolishly", and add marg. Or, *attributed folly to God*

III. 4 For "regard it from above" read "from above seek for it"
   11 For "when I" etc. read "when my mother bare me?"
   19 For "great" read "the great"
   24 For "roarings" read "groanings" and add marg. "Heb. *roarings.*"

IV. 4 For "confirmed" read "made firm"
   6 Read "*And* the integrity of thy ways thy hope?"

VI. 2 Read in the 2d line "And all my calamity laid in the balances!"
   10 Read "And be it still my consolation,
            Yea, let me exult in pain that spareth not," etc.
     3d line. Substitute the marg. ("*That*") for the text.
   13 For "effectual working" read "wisdom" and omit marg. So in xii, 16.
   25 Read "But your reproof, what doth it reprove?"
   26 For "imagine" read "think"

VII. 4 Substitute marg. ("*When shall I arise, and the night be gone?*") for the text.
   7 For "wind" read "a breath"
   17 For "thine heart" read "thy mind"

VIII. 17 For "heap" read "*stone*-heap"

IX. 19 Substitute marg. ("*If* we speak *of strength, lo*, he is *mighty !* ") for the text.

For "who will appoint me a time ?" read "who, *saith he*, will summon me ? "

X. 22 1st line; read "The land dark as midnight;"

2d line; for "*A land*" read "*The land*"

3d line; for "darkness" read "midnight" and add marg. Heb. *thick darkness*

XI. 6 For "That it" read "For he"

For "effectual working" read "understanding" and omit marg.

XII. 4 2d line; read "I who called upon God and he answered:"

23 For "destroyeth" read "he destroyeth"

2d line; read "He enlargeth the nations, and he leadeth them *captive*" and omit marg.

24 For "the heart of" read "understanding from"

XIII. 8 For "respect his person" read "show partiality to him" and omit marg.

10 For "respect persons" read "show partiality" and omit marg.

11 For "excellency" read "majesty"   So in xxxi, 23.

15 Read "Behold, he will slay me; I have no hope" and substitute the present text for marg.

16 Substitute marg. ("*That*") for the text, substituting a comma for the preceding semicolon.

18 For "ordered my cause" read "set my cause in order" So in xxiii, 4.

27 For "drawest thee a line about" read "settest a bound to"

XIV. 10 For "wasteth away" read "is laid low"

11 For "decayeth" read "wasteth"

19 For "And" read "So"

XV. 8 For "restrain" read "limit"

11 2d line; read "Even the word that is gentle toward thee"

12 For "wink" read "flash"

27 For "made collops of fat on his flanks" read "gathered fat upon his loins"

29 Let marg. ("*their possessions*" etc.) and the text exchange places.

XVII. 2 For "abideth in " read " dwelleth upon "
6 For " He hath made me also " read " But he hath made me "   .
For " And I am become an open abhorring " read " And they spit in my face " and omit marg.
XVIII. 12 Let marg. ("*at his side*") and the text exchange places.
13 Read "The members of his body shall be devoured "
XIX. 17 For " children of my *mother's* womb " read " children of mine own mother "
25, 26 Read
(25) " But as for me, I know that my redeemer liveth, And at last he shall stand up upon the earth ;
(26) And after my skin, *even* this *body*, is destroyed, Then without my flesh shall I see God : "
and put the present text of ver. 26 in the margin.
27 For " Whom I " read " Whom I, even I,"
Let marg. ("*on my side*") and the text exchange places.
Substitute marg. ("as *a stranger* ") for the text.
28 Substitute marg. ("*And that* ") for the text.
XXI. 14 For " Yet they said " read " And they say "
21 Omit " in the midst "
32 For " And shall keep " read " And men shall keep "
XXII. 14 Substitute marg. ("*on the vault* ") for the text.
XXIV. 4 For " hide themselves together " read " all hide themselves "
10 For " an-hungred " read " hungry "
12 For " imputeth it not for folly " read " regardeth not the folly "
XXVIII. 4 Omit "*that passeth by* "
17 For " the exchange thereof be " read " it be exchanged for "
XXIX. 6 For " rivers " read " streams "
XXXI. 2 For " of God from above " read " from God above "
For " of the Almighty from on high " read " from the Almighty on high "
18 For " I have been her guide " read " her have I guided "
31 For " satisfied " read " filled "
For " flesh " read " meat "   Omit marg.

XXXII. 19 For "belly" read "breast" and omit marg.

XXXIV. 20 Transpose "alike" to the beginning of the line.

XXXV. 6 1st line; for "doest" read "effectest"

XXXVI. 18 Read "For let not wrath stir thee up against chastisements" and put the present text in the marg.

XXXVII. 1 For "At this also" read "Yea, at this"

2 For "Hearken ye unto" read "Hear, oh, hear"

21 For "cleanseth" read "cleareth"

XXXVIII. 10 For "prescribed for it my decree" read "marked out for it my bound" and omit marg.

18 For "the breadth of the earth" read "the earth in its breadth"

30 Read "hide themselves *and become* like stone"

41 For "food" read "prey"

XXXIX. 5 2d line; For "wild ass" read "swift ass"

13 For "wing . . . rejoiceth" read "wings . . . wave proudly"

2d line, read "*But* are they the pinions and plumage of love?" with marg. to "love" Or, *a stork*

16 Let marg. ("*dealeth hardly with*") and the text exchange places.

28 Read "On the cliff she dwelleth and maketh her home, Upon the point of the cliff," etc.

XL. 15 For "with" read "as well as" and add marg. Heb. *with*

19 For "can make his sword to approach *unto him*" read "giveth him his sword" and omit marg.

XLI. 12 For "comely proportion" read "goodly frame"

18 For "neesings" read "sneezings"

APPENDIX II.

A BIBLIOGRAPHY OF THE BOOK OF JOB.

BY REV. S. G. AYRES

(*Assistant Librarian in Drew Theological Seminary*).

This brief Bibliography does not profess to be exhaustive, although the endeavor has been to make the list of English versions as nearly complete as is possible.

I.—VERSIONS AND PARAPHRASES.

BELLAMY, D.   A Paraphrase of Job.   4to.   London, 1748.

BRETT, ARTHUR.   Patientia Victrix; or, The Book of Job in Lyrick Verse.   16mo.   London, 1661.

CAREY, C. P.   The Book of Job Translated, Explained by Notes, and Illustrated by Extracts from Works on Antiquities, Science, etc. Royal 8vo.   1858.   The notes are critical and exegetical.

COLEMAN, J. N.   The Book of Job; from the Hebrew, with notes.   4to.   London, 1869.

CONANT, T. J., D.D.   The Book of Job.   A Translation from the Original Hebrew.   4to.   New York, 1867.   This is the American Union Version.

FRY, JOHN.   A New Translation and Exposition of the Book of Job, with Notes.   8vo.   London, 1837.

GARDEN, CHARLES, D.D.   An Improved Metrical Version of the Book of Job, with Preliminary Dissertation and Notes.   8vo.   Oxford, 1796.

GENUNG, JOHN F.   The Epic of the Inner Life.   Being the Book of Job Translated Anew.   16mo.   Boston, 1890.

GOOD, JOHN MASON, M.D., F.R.S.   The Book of Job Literally Translated, with Notes, etc.   8vo.   London, 1812.

LEE, SAMUEL, D.D.   The Book of Job Translated, with Introduction and Commentary.   8vo.   London, 1837.

NOYES, G. R. A New Translation of the Book of Job, with Notes. 12mo. Boston, n. d.

SCOTT, THOMAS. The Book of Job in English Verse, with Remarks. 4to. London, 1771.

SENAULT, J. F. A Paraphrase on the Book of Job. 4to. London, 1648.

STATTER, LIEUTENANT-COLONEL W. C. The Book of Job in English Verse, with Notes. 12mo. London, 1859.

STOCK, JOSEPH, D.D. The Book of Job Metrically Arranged and Newly Translated, with Notes. 4to. London, 1805.

UMBREIT, D. F. W. New Version of the Book of Job, with Expository Notes. 2 vols. 12mo. Edinburgh, 1836.

WEMYS, THOMAS. Job and His Times. A New Version with Notes. 8vo. London, 1839. The best part of this book is the review of the "State of the Arts and Sciences in Job's Day."

II.—COMMENTARIES.

CARYL, JOSEPH. Exposition of the Book of Job, with Practical Observations. 12 vols., 4to. 1648. Also in 2 vols., folio. 1676. This is the most exhaustive work on the subject. An abridged edition was published at Edinburgh in 1836.

CHEYNE, T. K. Job and Solomon. 12mo. New York, 1887.

CROLY, G. The Book of Job. 12mo. Edinburgh, 1863.

CURRY, DANIEL, D.D., LL.D. The Book of Job. 12mo. New York, 1887.

DAVIDSON, A. B. A Commentary on Job, Grammatical and Exegetical, with a Translation. 8vo. London, 1862. This, though not as exhaustive as Caryl, for practical purposes is the best of all. It is thoroughly critical.

EWALD, H. Commentary on the Book of Job. Translated by Rev. J. F. Smith. 8vo. London, 1882.

HUTCHESON, GEORGE. An Exposition upon Job. Being the sum of three hundred and sixteen lectures. Folio. London, 1669. Spurgeon says that this book is a very helpful one.

PETERS, CHARLES. A Critical Dissertation on the Book of Job. 4to. London, 1751.

THOMAS, REV. D. Problemati Mundi: The Book of Job Exegetically and Practically Considered. 8vo. London, 1879.

VAN HAGEN, MRS. HENRY. Evenings in the Land of Uz : A Comment on Job. Second edition, 12mo. London, 1843.

See also in the collected commentaries of Barnes, Benson, Calvin, Clarke, Cowles, Delitzsch, Scott, and Wesley; as well as in the Bible Commentary and the Pulpit Commentary.

III.—ESSAYS.

CARLYLE, THOMAS. Heroes and Hero Worship. 12mo. New York, 1849. Lecture II, p. 44.

FLOY, REV. JAMES, D.D. Old Testament Characters. 12mo. New York, 1866. Pp. 314-342.

FROUDE, JAMES A. Short Studies on Great Subjects. Vol. i, pp. 228-274. 12mo. New York, 1868.

GILFILLAN, GEORGE. The Bards of the Bible. 12mo. New York, 1851. Chapter V, Poetry of the Book of Job.

GREEN, W. H. The Arguments of the Book of Job Unfolded. 12mo. New York, 1874. Chapter II discusses Satan. The book closes with an analysis.

HODGES, WALTER. Elihu: An Inquiry into the Scope and Design of the Book of Job. 4to. London, 1750. 12mo, 3d edition, 1756. He tries to show that Job is a type of the Saviour, and that Elihu was the Son of God himself.

KITTO, JOHN. "Job and the Poetical Books" in daily Bible illustrations.

IV.—SERMONS.

CALVIN, JOHN. Sermons on the Book of Job. Translated out of the French by A. Golding. Folio. London, 1584. Not the same as the Commentary.

EVANS, A. B. Lectures on the Book of Job. 8vo. London, 1856. Sermons on fourteen single verses from different parts of the book.

HULBERT, A. C. Sermons. 12mo. London, 1853.

WAGNER, GEORGE. Sermons on the Book of Job. Crown, 8vo. London, 1863.